Jim Henson's™ FRAGGLE ROCK™

THE ROUGH SIDE OF THE ROCK

Published by
ARCHAIA™

Series Designer **MICHELLE ANKLEY**
Collection Designer **JILLIAN CRAB**
Assistant Editor **GAVIN GRONENTHAL**
Editor **CAMERON CHITTOCK**

JIM HENSON'S FRAGGLE ROCK: THE ROUGH SIDE OF THE ROCK, April 2019. Published by Archaia, a division of Boom Entertainment, Inc. © 2019 The Jim Henson Company. JIM HENSON's mark & logo, FRAGGLE ROCK, mark & logo, and all related characters and elements are trademarks of The Jim Henson Company. Originally published in single magazine form as JIM HENSON'S FRAGGLE ROCK No. 2. ™ & © 2018 The Jim Henson Company. All Rights Reserved. Archaia™ and the Archaia logo are trademarks of Boom Entertainment, Inc., registered in various countries and categories. All characters, events, and institutions depicted herein are fictional. Any similarity between any of the names, characters, persons, events, and/or institutions in this publication to actual names, characters, and persons, whether living or dead, events, and/or institutions is unintended and purely coincidental.

BOOM! Studios, 5670 Wilshire Boulevard, Suite 400, Los Angeles, CA 90036-5679. Printed in China. First Printing.

ISBN: 978-1-68415-335-0, eISBN: 978-1-64144-188-9

Jim Henson's™

FRAGGLE ROCK™

THE ROUGH SIDE OF THE ROCK

Story and Art by
JAY FOSGITT

Colors by
JOANA LAFUENTE

Letters by
MIKE FIORENTINO

Cover Art by
JAY FOSGITT

Special Thanks to
BRIAN HENSON, LISA HENSON, JIM FORMANEK, NICOLE GOLDMAN, CARLA DELLAVEDOVA, KAREN FALK, BLANCA LISTA, SHANE MANG,
and the entire Jim Henson Company team.

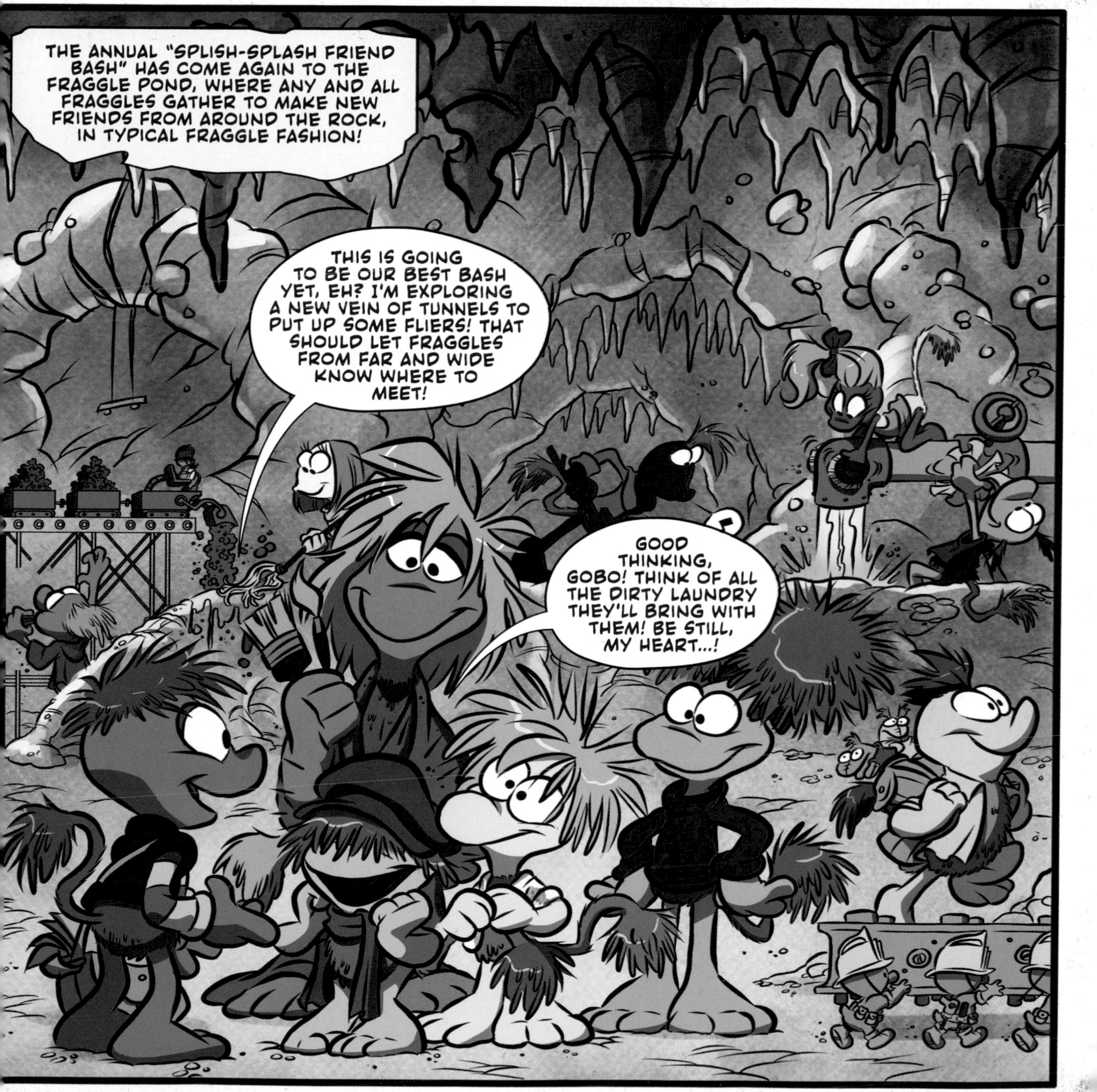
THE ANNUAL "SPLISH-SPLASH FRIEND BASH" HAS COME AGAIN TO THE FRAGGLE POND, WHERE ANY AND ALL FRAGGLES GATHER TO MAKE NEW FRIENDS FROM AROUND THE ROCK, IN TYPICAL FRAGGLE FASHION!
THIS IS GOING TO BE OUR BEST BASH YET, EH? I'M EXPLORING A NEW VEIN OF TUNNELS TO PUT UP SOME FLIERS! THAT SHOULD LET FRAGGLES FROM FAR AND WIDE KNOW WHERE TO MEET!
GOOD THINKING, GOBO! THINK OF ALL THE DIRTY LAUNDRY THEY'LL BRING WITH THEM! BE STILL, MY HEART...!

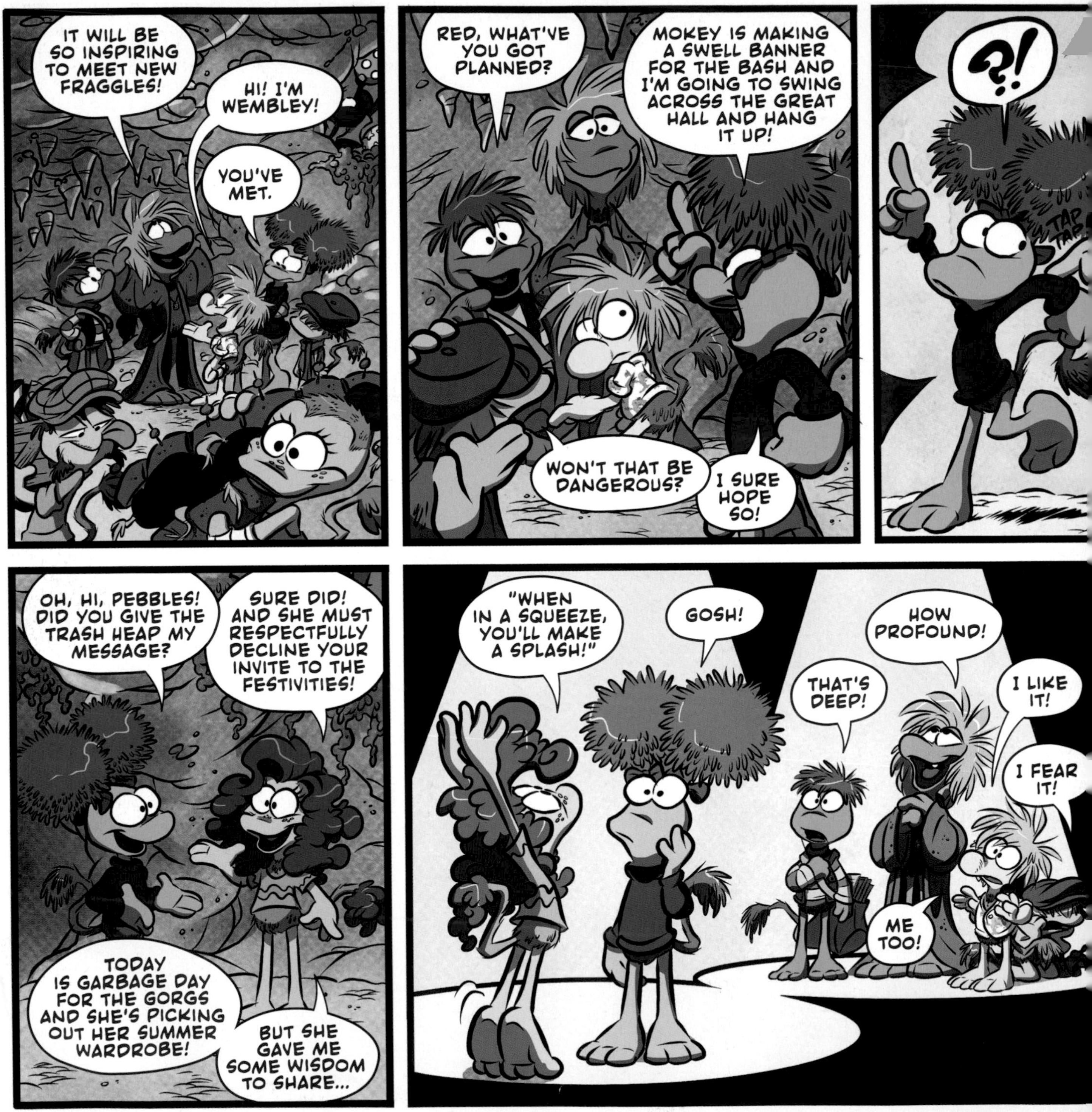
IT WILL BE SO INSPIRING TO MEET NEW FRAGGLES!
HI! I'M WEMBLEY!
YOU'VE MET.
RED, WHAT'VE YOU GOT PLANNED?
MOKEY IS MAKING A SWELL BANNER FOR THE BASH AND I'M GOING TO SWING ACROSS THE GREAT HALL AND HANG IT UP!
WON'T THAT BE DANGEROUS?
I SURE HOPE SO!
?!
TAP TAP
OH, HI, PEBBLES! DID YOU GIVE THE TRASH HEAP MY MESSAGE?
SURE DID! AND SHE MUST RESPECTFULLY DECLINE YOUR INVITE TO THE FESTIVITIES!
TODAY IS GARBAGE DAY FOR THE GORGS AND SHE'S PICKING OUT HER SUMMER WARDROBE!
BUT SHE GAVE ME SOME WISDOM TO SHARE...
"WHEN IN A SQUEEZE, YOU'LL MAKE A SPLASH!"
GOSH!
THAT'S DEEP!
HOW PROFOUND!
I LIKE IT!
I FEAR IT!
ME TOO!

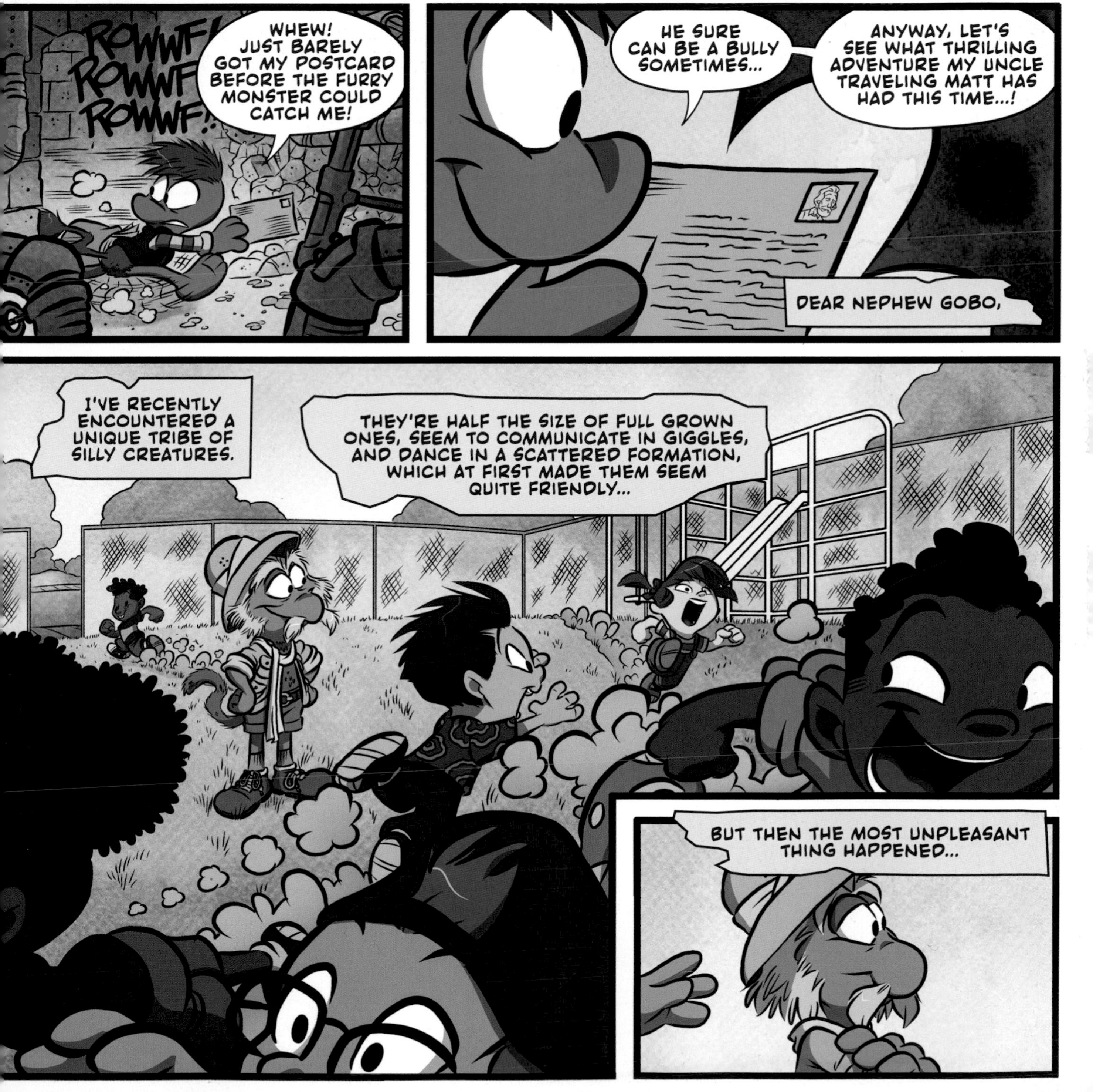
ROWWF! ROWWF! ROWWF!
WHEW! JUST BARELY GOT MY POSTCARD BEFORE THE FURRY MONSTER COULD CATCH ME!
HE SURE CAN BE A BULLY SOMETIMES...
ANYWAY, LET'S SEE WHAT THRILLING ADVENTURE MY UNCLE TRAVELING MATT HAS HAD THIS TIME...!
DEAR NEPHEW GOBO,
I'VE RECENTLY ENCOUNTERED A UNIQUE TRIBE OF SILLY CREATURES.
THEY'RE HALF THE SIZE OF FULL GROWN ONES, SEEM TO COMMUNICATE IN GIGGLES, AND DANCE IN A SCATTERED FORMATION, WHICH AT FIRST MADE THEM SEEM QUITE FRIENDLY...
BUT THEN THE MOST UNPLEASANT THING HAPPENED...

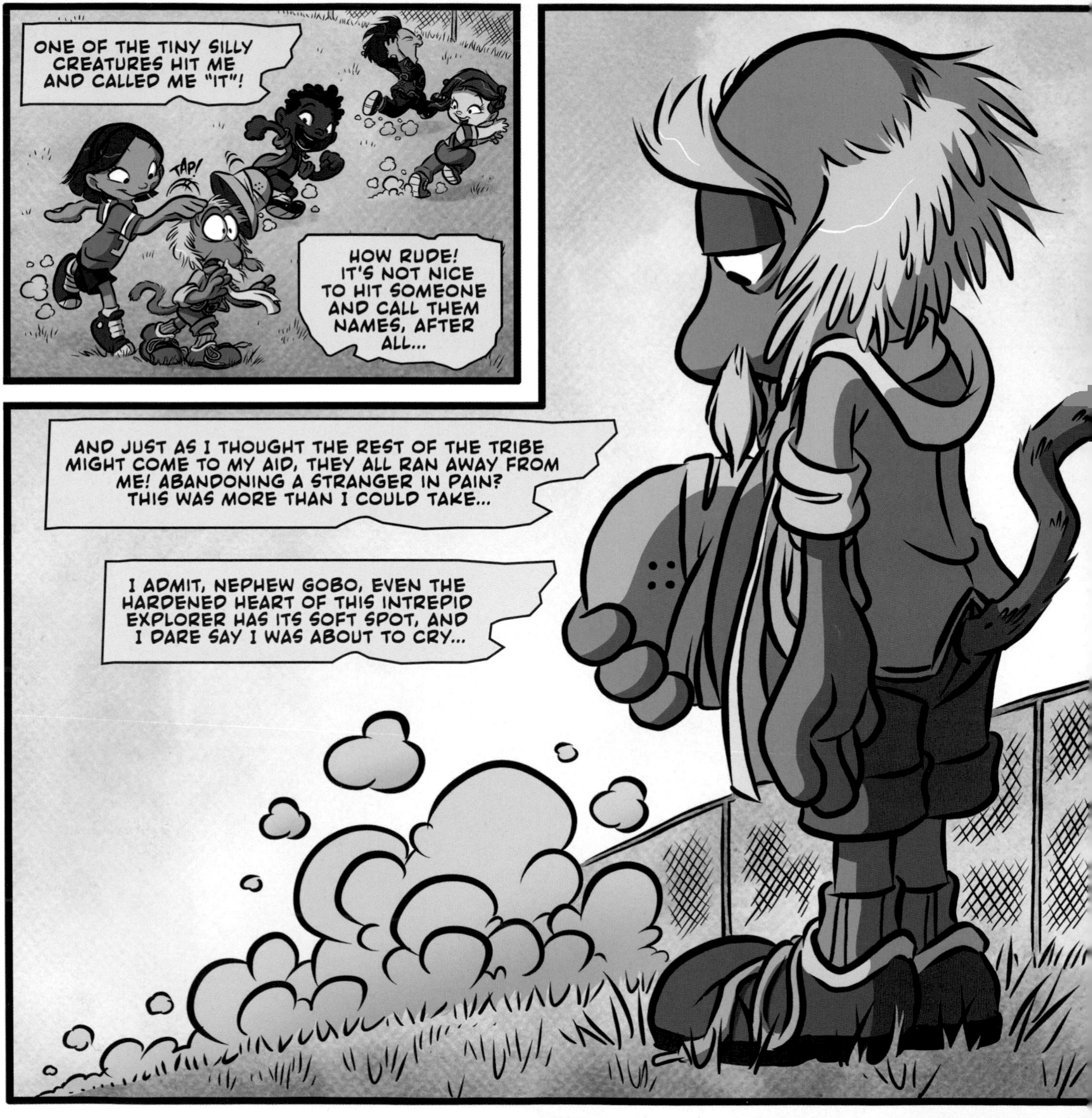
ONE OF THE TINY SILLY CREATURES HIT ME AND CALLED ME "IT"!
TAP!
HOW RUDE! IT'S NOT NICE TO HIT SOMEONE AND CALL THEM NAMES, AFTER ALL...
AND JUST AS I THOUGHT THE REST OF THE TRIBE MIGHT COME TO MY AID, THEY ALL RAN AWAY FROM ME! ABANDONING A STRANGER IN PAIN? THIS WAS MORE THAN I COULD TAKE...
I ADMIT, NEPHEW GOBO, EVEN THE HARDENED HEART OF THIS INTREPID EXPLORER HAS ITS SOFT SPOT, AND I DARE SAY I WAS ABOUT TO CRY...

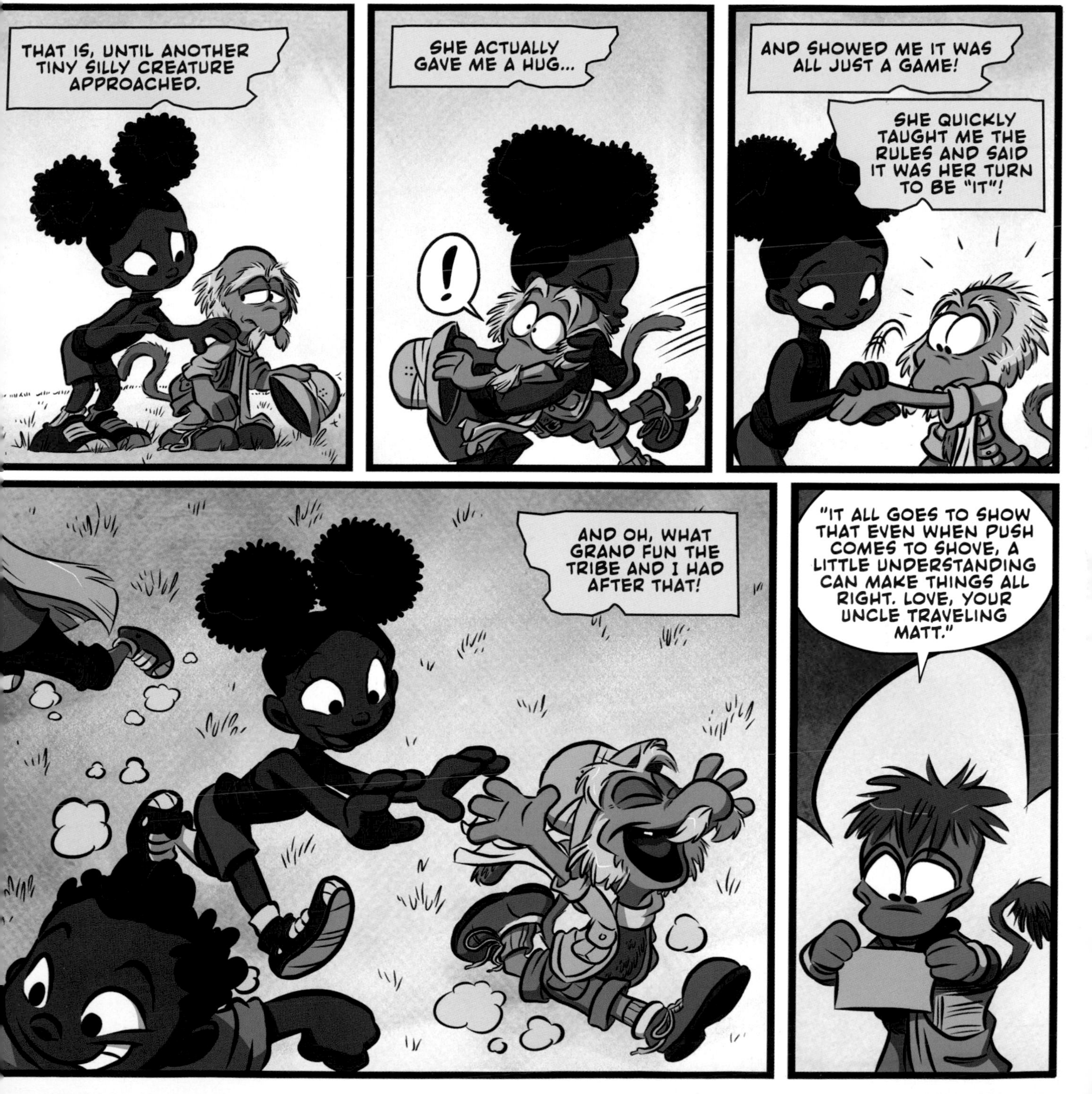
THAT IS, UNTIL ANOTHER TINY SILLY CREATURE APPROACHED.
SHE ACTUALLY GAVE ME A HUG...
!
AND SHOWED ME IT WAS ALL JUST A GAME!
SHE QUICKLY TAUGHT ME THE RULES AND SAID IT WAS HER TURN TO BE "IT"!
AND OH, WHAT GRAND FUN THE TRIBE AND I HAD AFTER THAT!
"IT ALL GOES TO SHOW THAT EVEN WHEN PUSH COMES TO SHOVE, A LITTLE UNDERSTANDING CAN MAKE THINGS ALL RIGHT. LOVE, YOUR UNCLE TRAVELING MATT."

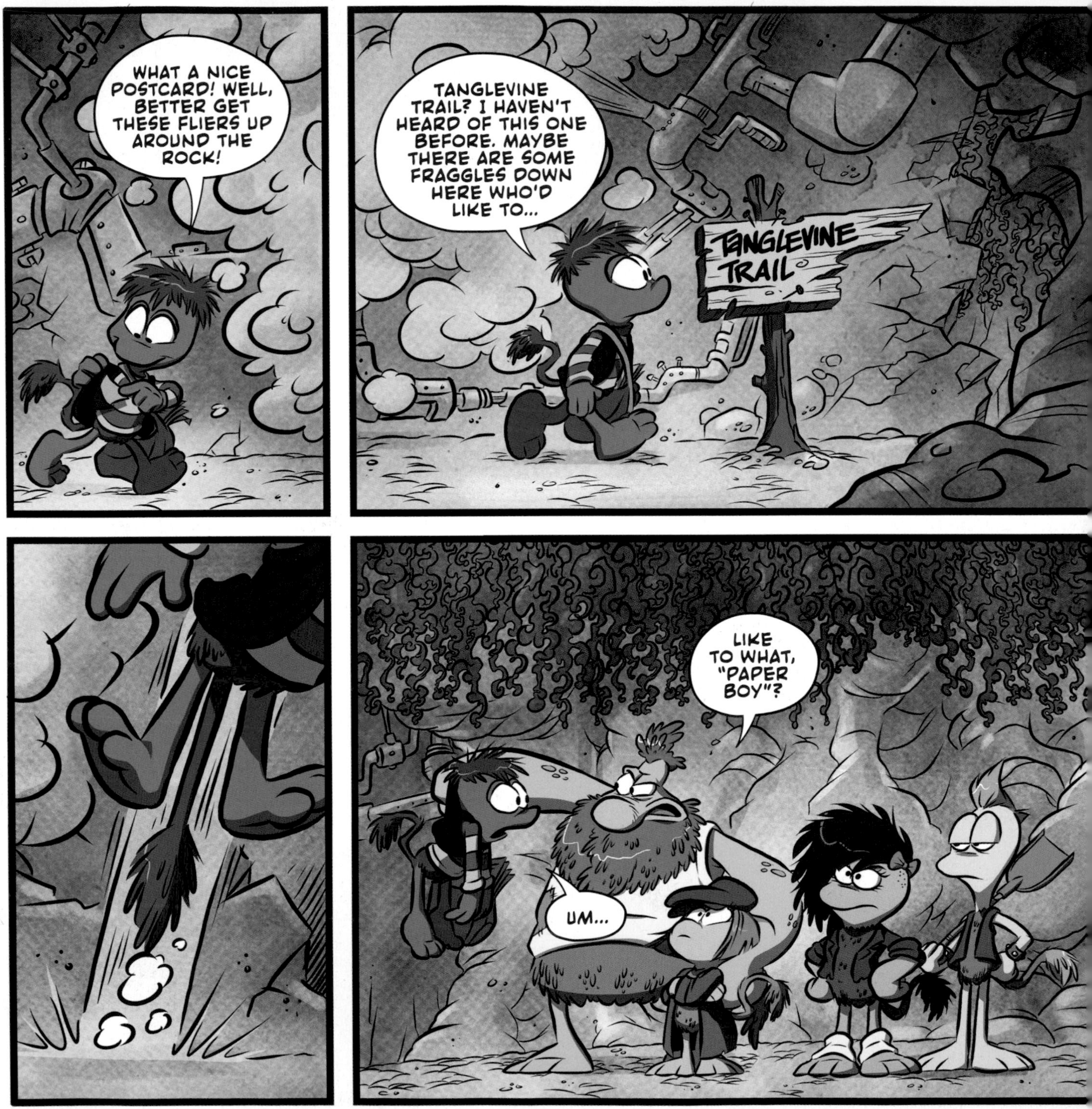
WHAT A NICE POSTCARD! WELL, BETTER GET THESE FLIERS UP AROUND THE ROCK!
TANGLEVINE TRAIL? I HAVEN'T HEARD OF THIS ONE BEFORE. MAYBE THERE ARE SOME FRAGGLES DOWN HERE WHO'D LIKE TO...
TANGLEVINE TRAIL
LIKE TO WHAT, "PAPER BOY"?
UM...

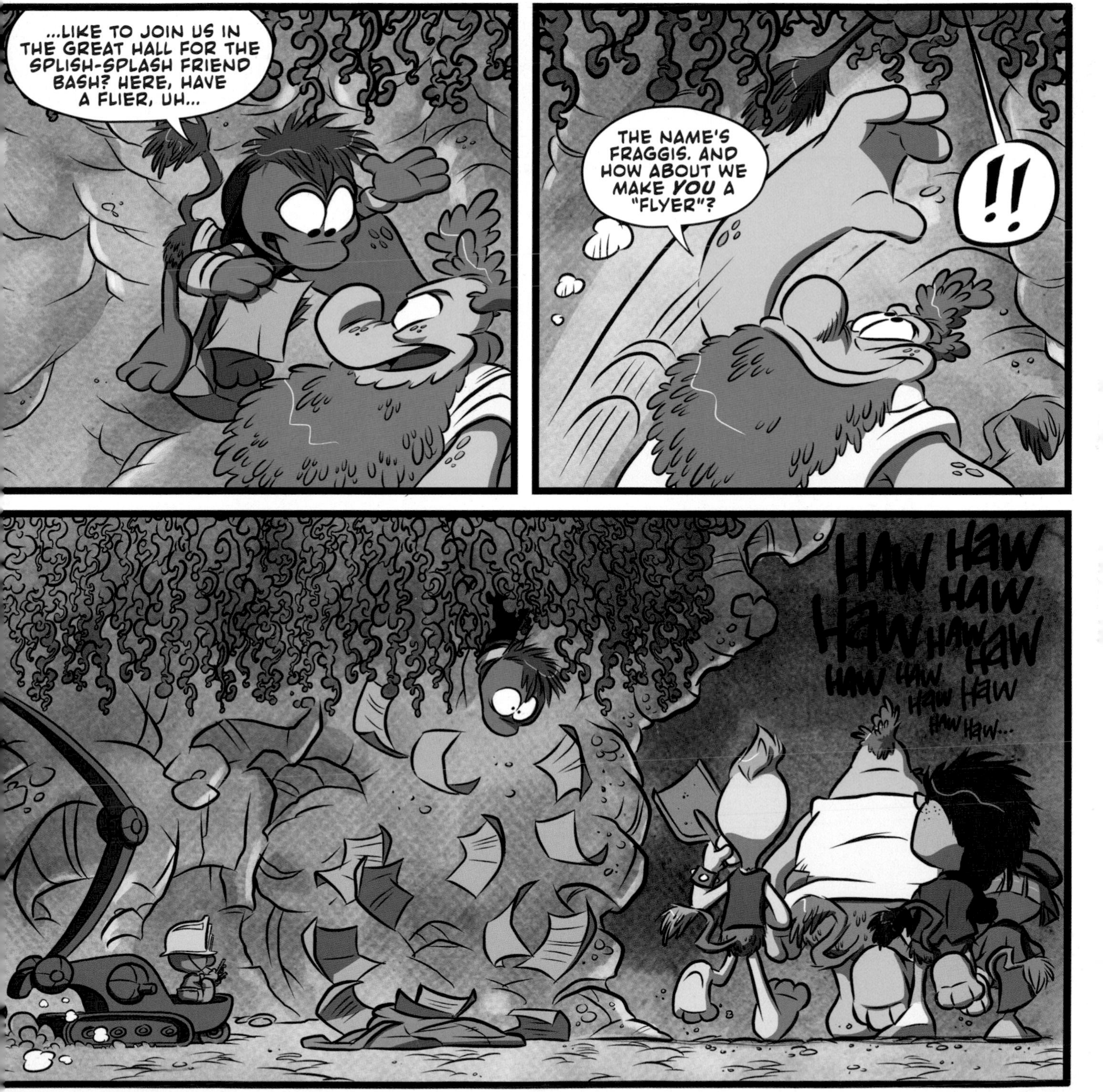
...LIKE TO JOIN US IN THE GREAT HALL FOR THE SPLISH-SPLASH FRIEND BASH? HERE, HAVE A FLIER, UH...
THE NAME'S FRAGGIS. AND HOW ABOUT WE MAKE *YOU* A "FLYER"?
!!
HAW HAW
HAW
HAW HAW HAW
HAW HAW HAW
HAW HAW
HAW HAW...

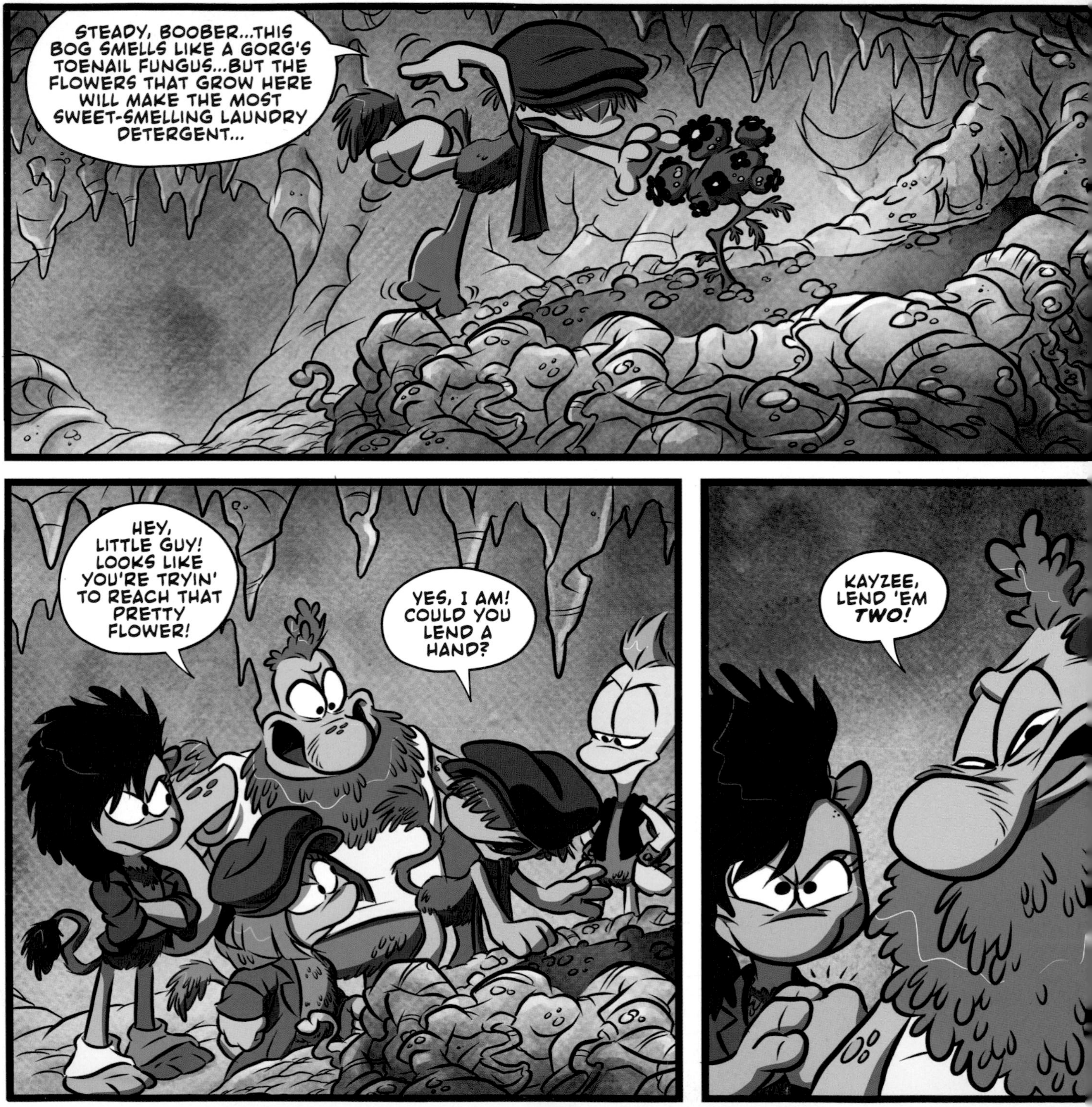
STEADY, BOOBER...THIS BOG SMELLS LIKE A GORG'S TOENAIL FUNGUS...BUT THE FLOWERS THAT GROW HERE WILL MAKE THE MOST SWEET-SMELLING LAUNDRY DETERGENT...
HEY, LITTLE GUY! LOOKS LIKE YOU'RE TRYIN' TO REACH THAT PRETTY FLOWER!
YES, I AM! COULD YOU LEND A HAND?
KAYZEE, LEND 'EM TWO!

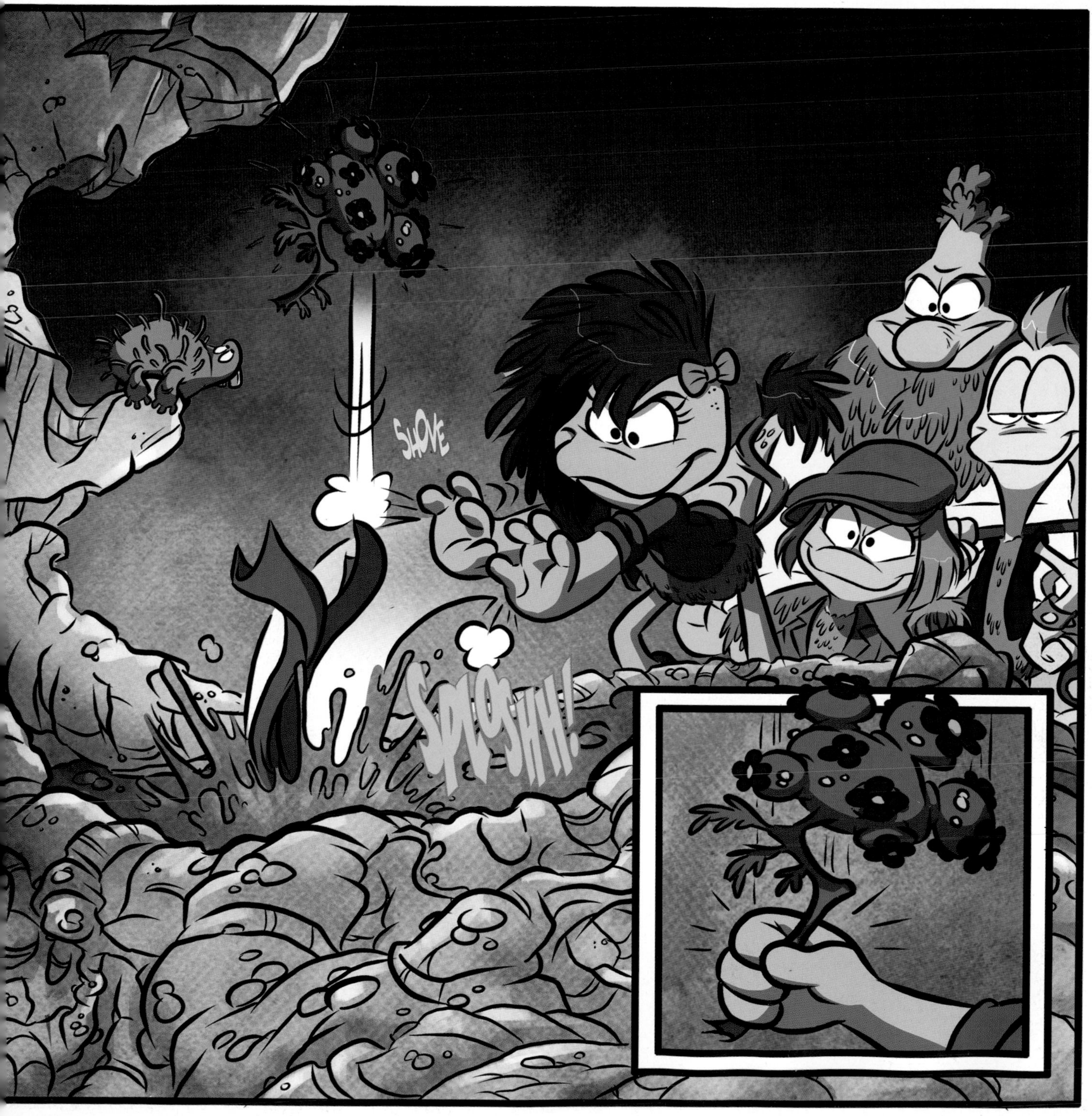
SHOVE
SPLOSHH!

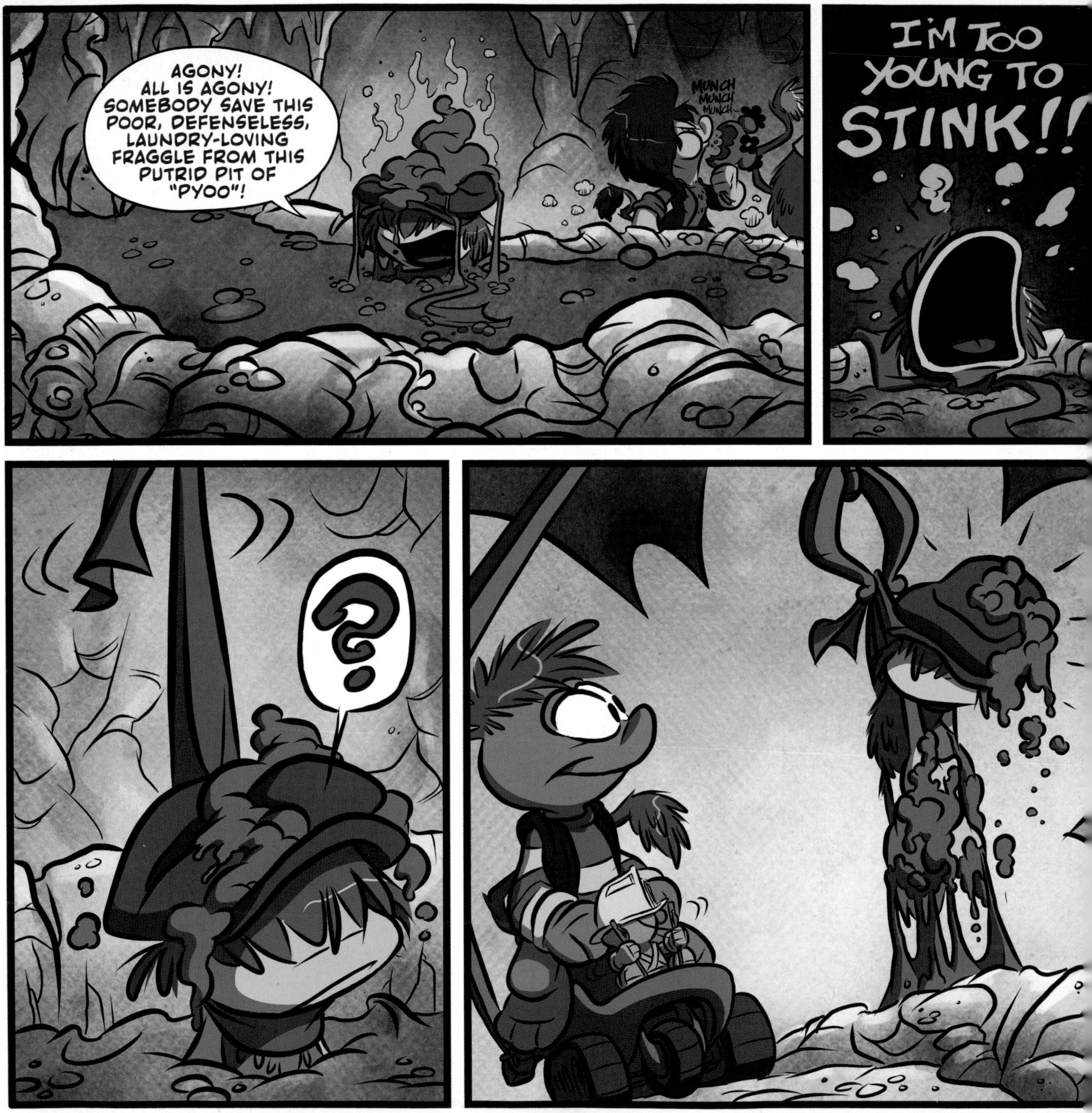
AGONY! ALL IS AGONY! SOMEBODY SAVE THIS POOR, DEFENSELESS, LAUNDRY-LOVING FRAGGLE FROM THIS PUTRID PIT OF "PYOO"!
MUNCH MUNCH MUNCH...
I'M TOO YOUNG TO STINK!!
?

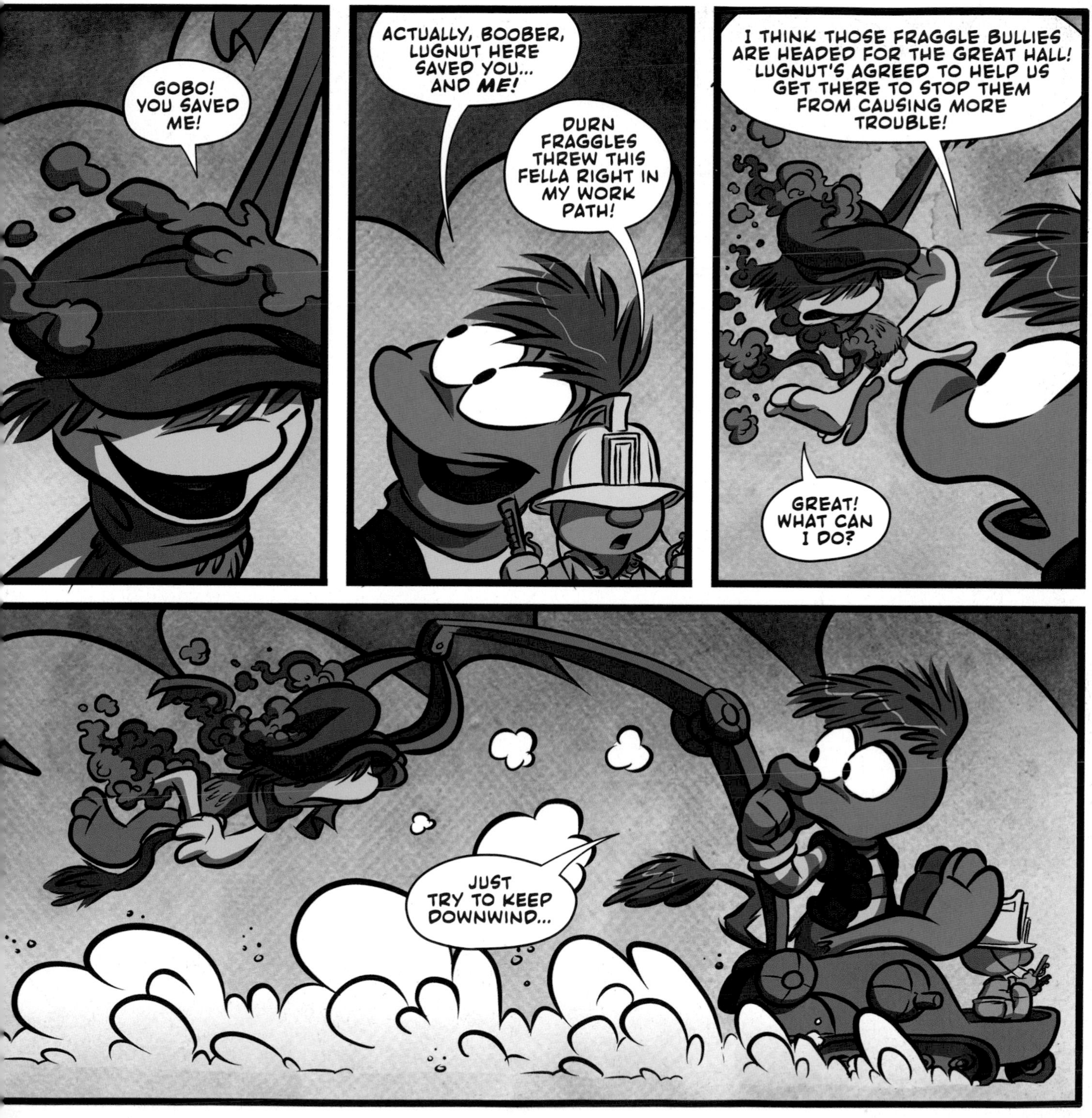
GOBO! YOU SAVED ME!
ACTUALLY, BOOBER, LUGNUT HERE SAVED YOU... AND *ME!*
DURN FRAGGLES THREW THIS FELLA RIGHT IN MY WORK PATH!
I THINK THOSE FRAGGLE BULLIES ARE HEADED FOR THE GREAT HALL! LUGNUT'S AGREED TO HELP US GET THERE TO STOP THEM FROM CAUSING MORE TROUBLE!
GREAT! WHAT CAN I DO?
JUST TRY TO KEEP DOWNWIND...

BACK IN THE GREAT HALL...

MOKEY, WHAT CAN I DO? EVERYONE HAS SOMETHING TO DO FOR THE SPLISH-SPLASH FRIEND BASH BUT ME!

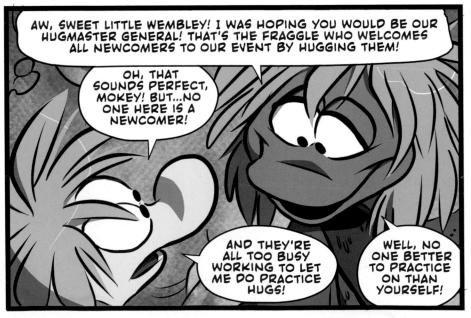

AW, SWEET LITTLE WEMBLEY! I WAS HOPING YOU WOULD BE OUR HUGMASTER GENERAL! THAT'S THE FRAGGLE WHO WELCOMES ALL NEWCOMERS TO OUR EVENT BY HUGGING THEM!

OH, THAT SOUNDS PERFECT, MOKEY! BUT...NO ONE HERE IS A NEWCOMER!

AND THEY'RE ALL TOO BUSY WORKING TO LET ME DO PRACTICE HUGS!

WELL, NO ONE BETTER TO PRACTICE ON THAN YOURSELF!

WHY DIDN'T I THINK OF THAT?

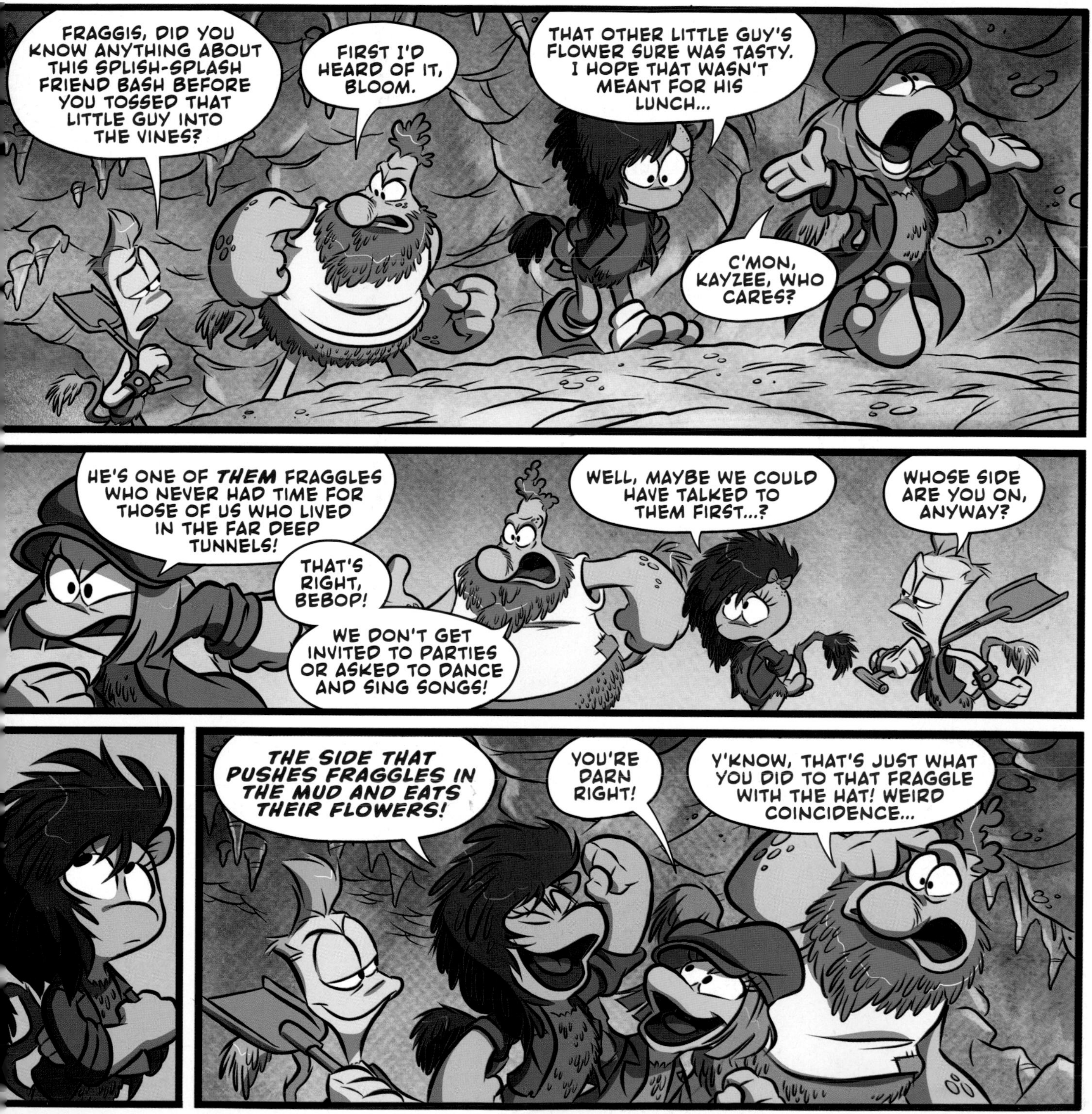
FRAGGIS, DID YOU KNOW ANYTHING ABOUT THIS SPLISH-SPLASH FRIEND BASH BEFORE YOU TOSSED THAT LITTLE GUY INTO THE VINES?
FIRST I'D HEARD OF IT, BLOOM.
THAT OTHER LITTLE GUY'S FLOWER SURE WAS TASTY. I HOPE THAT WASN'T MEANT FOR HIS LUNCH...
C'MON, KAYZEE, WHO CARES?
HE'S ONE OF *THEM* FRAGGLES WHO NEVER HAD TIME FOR THOSE OF US WHO LIVED IN THE FAR DEEP TUNNELS!
THAT'S RIGHT, BEBOP!
WE DON'T GET INVITED TO PARTIES OR ASKED TO DANCE AND SING SONGS!
WELL, MAYBE WE COULD HAVE TALKED TO THEM FIRST...?
WHOSE SIDE ARE YOU ON, ANYWAY?
THE SIDE THAT PUSHES FRAGGLES IN THE MUD AND EATS THEIR FLOWERS!
YOU'RE DARN RIGHT!
Y'KNOW, THAT'S JUST WHAT YOU DID TO THAT FRAGGLE WITH THE HAT! WEIRD COINCIDENCE...

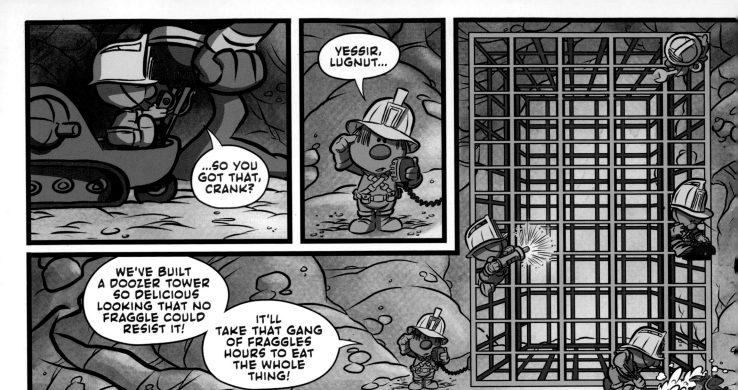

...SO YOU GOT THAT, CRANK?

YESSIR, LUGNUT...

WE'VE BUILT A DOOZER TOWER SO DELICIOUS LOOKING THAT NO FRAGGLE COULD RESIST IT!

IT'LL TAKE THAT GANG OF FRAGGLES HOURS TO EAT THE WHOLE THING!

THANKS, CRANK. WE WOULD HAVE BEEN THERE TO HELP YOU...

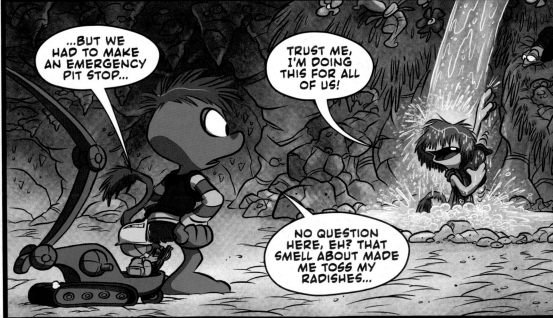

...BUT WE HAD TO MAKE AN EMERGENCY PIT STOP...

TRUST ME, I'M DOING THIS FOR ALL OF US!

NO QUESTION HERE, EH? THAT SMELL ABOUT MADE ME TOSS MY RADISHES...

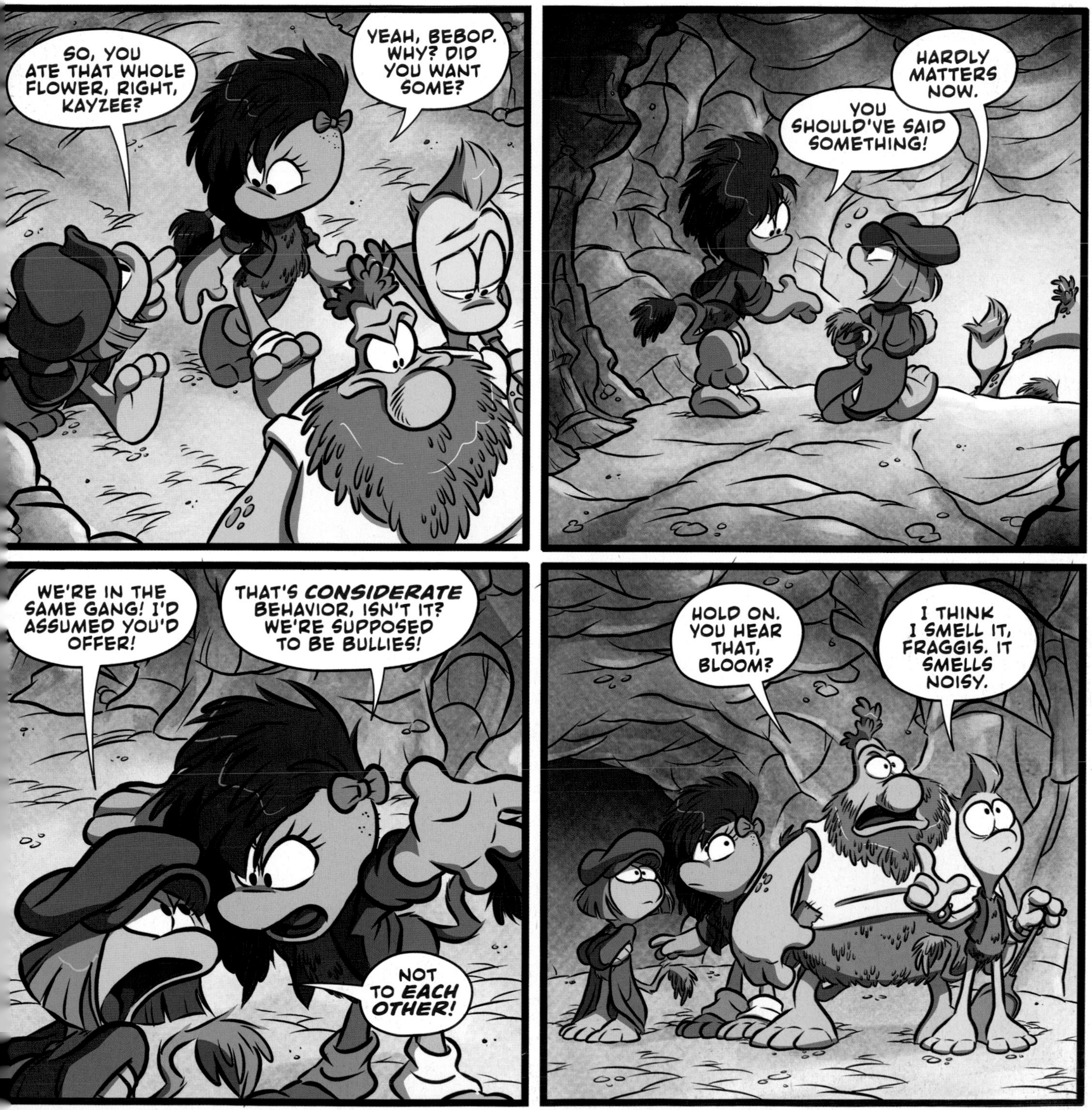
SO, YOU ATE THAT WHOLE FLOWER, RIGHT, KAYZEE?
YEAH, BEBOP. WHY? DID YOU WANT SOME?
YOU SHOULD'VE SAID SOMETHING!
HARDLY MATTERS NOW.
WE'RE IN THE SAME GANG! I'D ASSUMED YOU'D OFFER!
THAT'S *CONSIDERATE* BEHAVIOR, ISN'T IT? WE'RE SUPPOSED TO BE BULLIES!
NOT TO *EACH OTHER!*
HOLD ON. YOU HEAR THAT, BLOOM?
I THINK I SMELL IT, FRAGGIS. IT SMELLS NOISY.

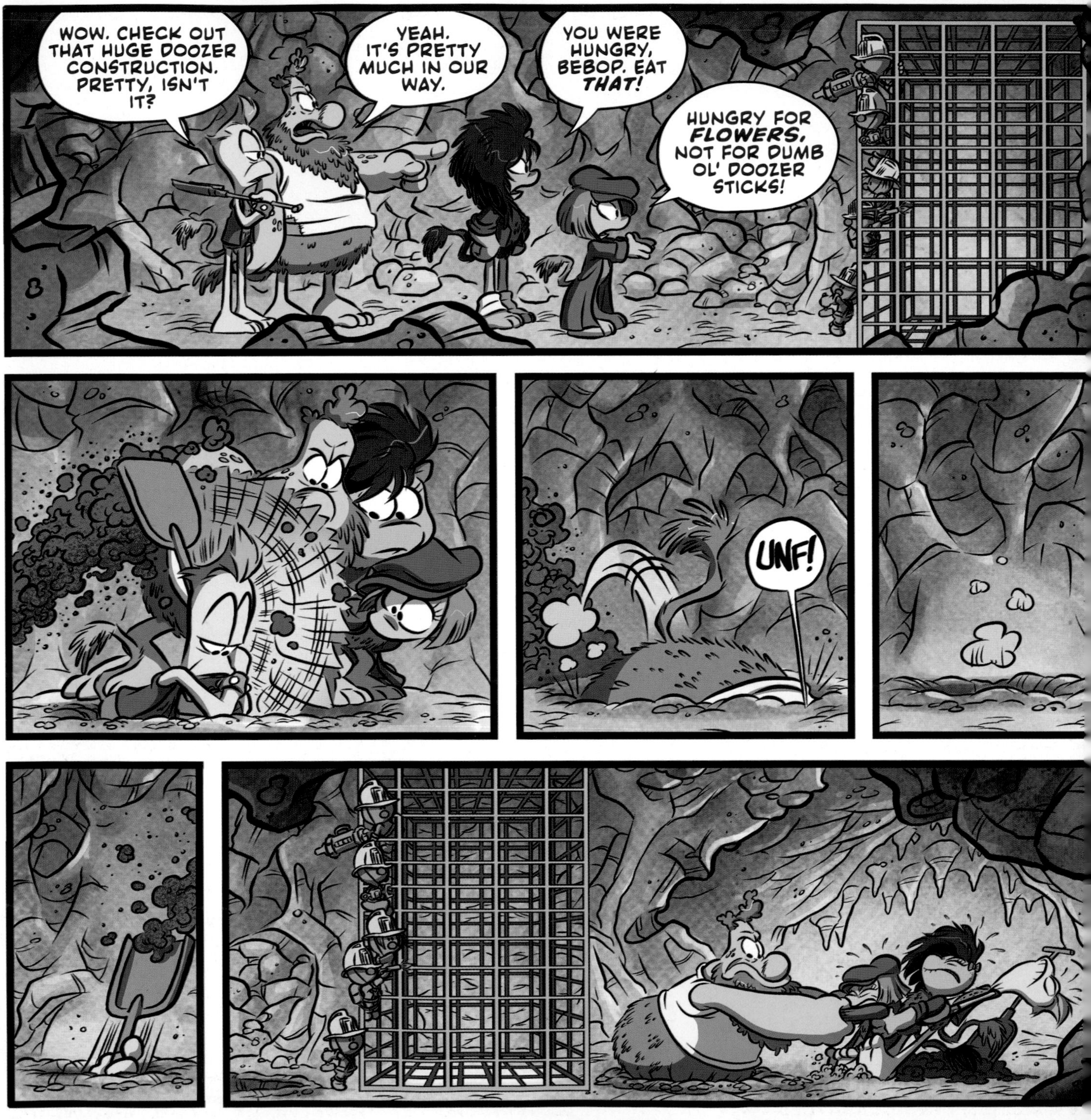
WOW. CHECK OUT THAT HUGE DOOZER CONSTRUCTION. PRETTY, ISN'T IT?
YEAH. IT'S PRETTY MUCH IN OUR WAY.
YOU WERE HUNGRY, BEBOP. EAT *THAT!*
HUNGRY FOR ***FLOWERS,*** NOT FOR DUMB OL' DOOZER STICKS!
UNF!

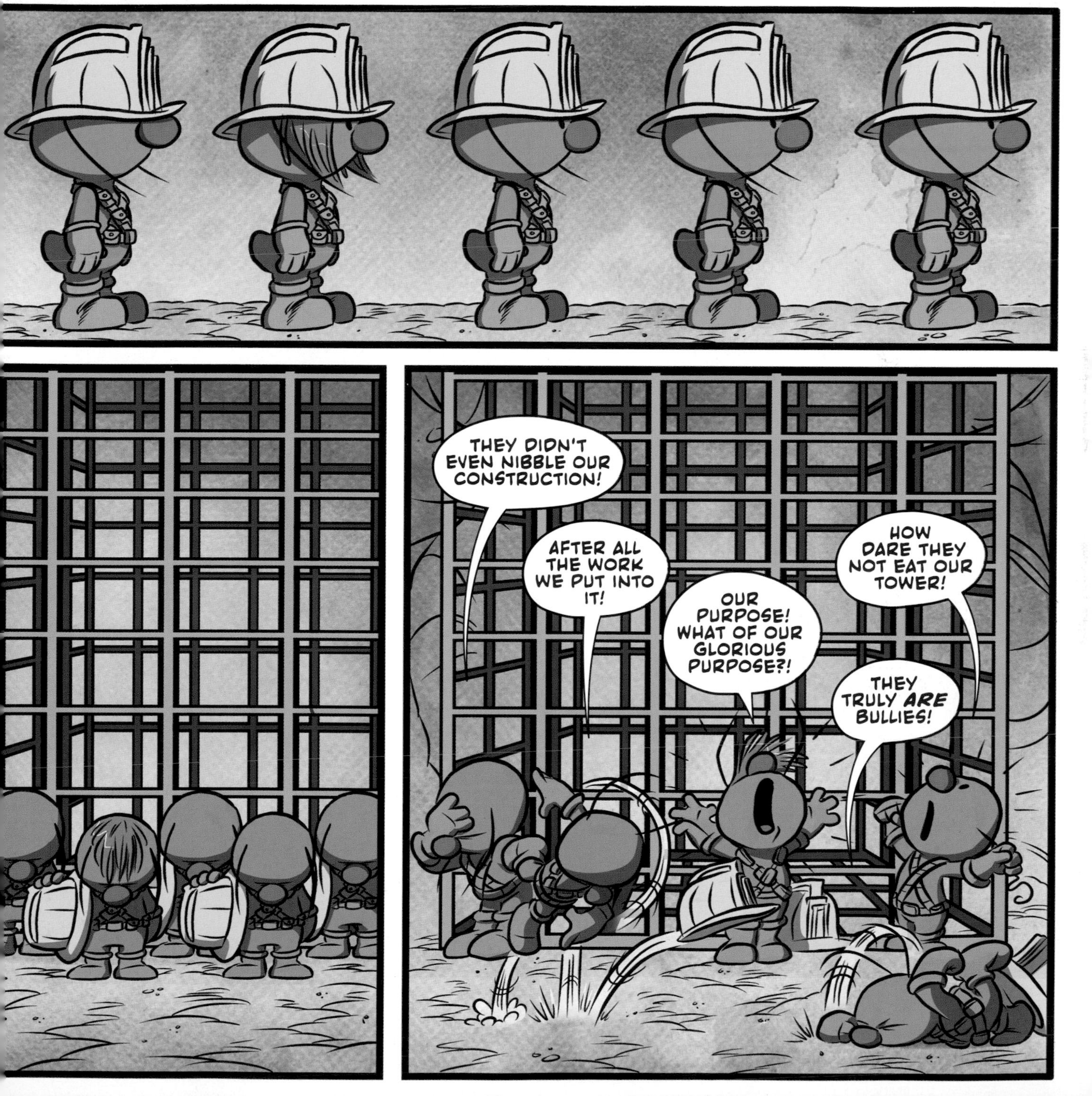
THEY DIDN'T EVEN NIBBLE OUR CONSTRUCTION!
AFTER ALL THE WORK WE PUT INTO IT!
OUR PURPOSE! WHAT OF OUR GLORIOUS PURPOSE?!
HOW DARE THEY NOT EAT OUR TOWER!
THEY TRULY *ARE* BULLIES!

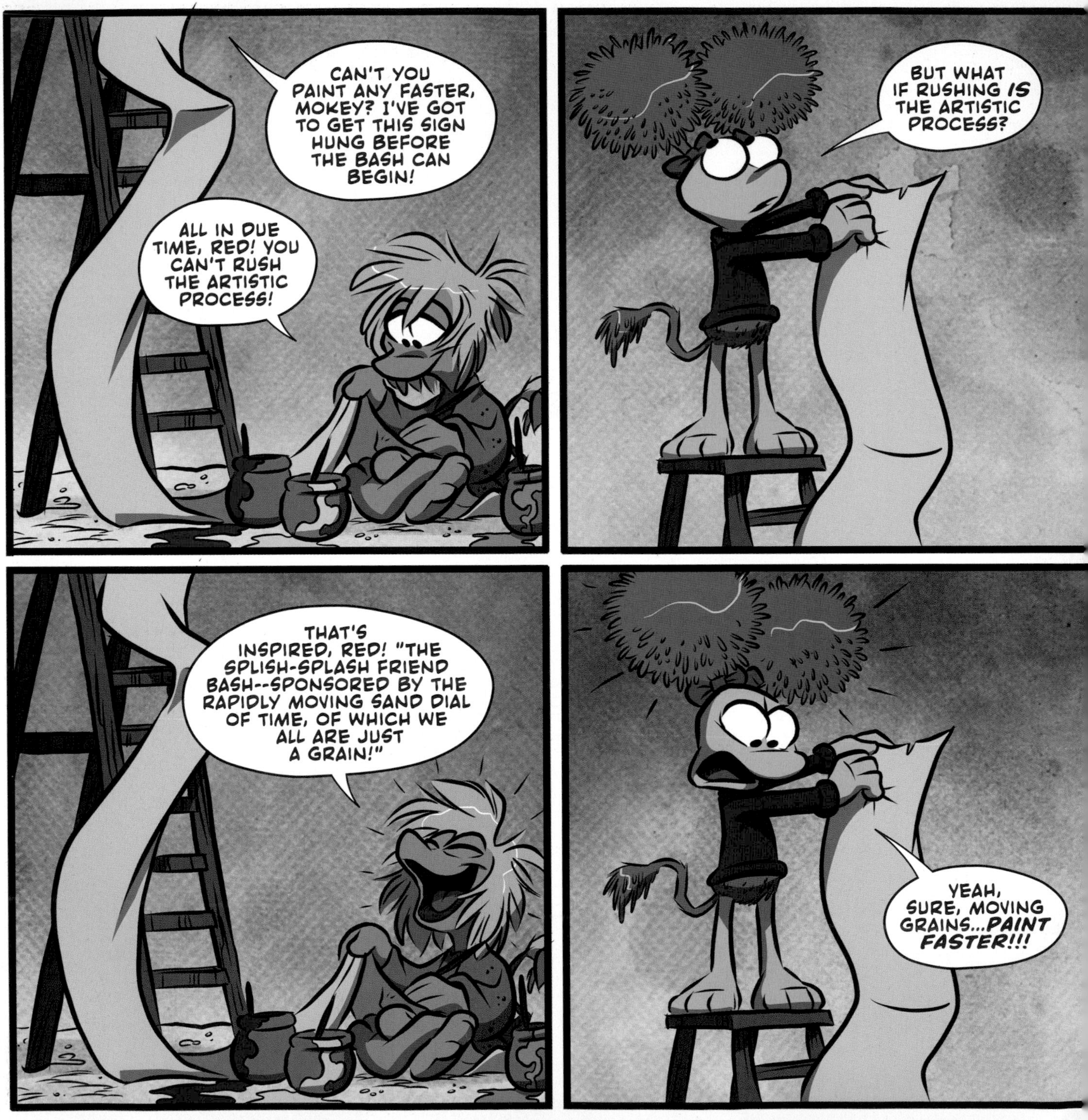
CAN'T YOU PAINT ANY FASTER, MOKEY? I'VE GOT TO GET THIS SIGN HUNG BEFORE THE BASH CAN BEGIN!
ALL IN DUE TIME, RED! YOU CAN'T RUSH THE ARTISTIC PROCESS!
BUT WHAT IF RUSHING *IS* THE ARTISTIC PROCESS?
THAT'S INSPIRED, RED! "THE SPLISH-SPLASH FRIEND BASH--SPONSORED BY THE RAPIDLY MOVING SAND DIAL OF TIME, OF WHICH WE ALL ARE JUST A GRAIN!"
YEAH, SURE, MOVING GRAINS...*PAINT FASTER!!!*

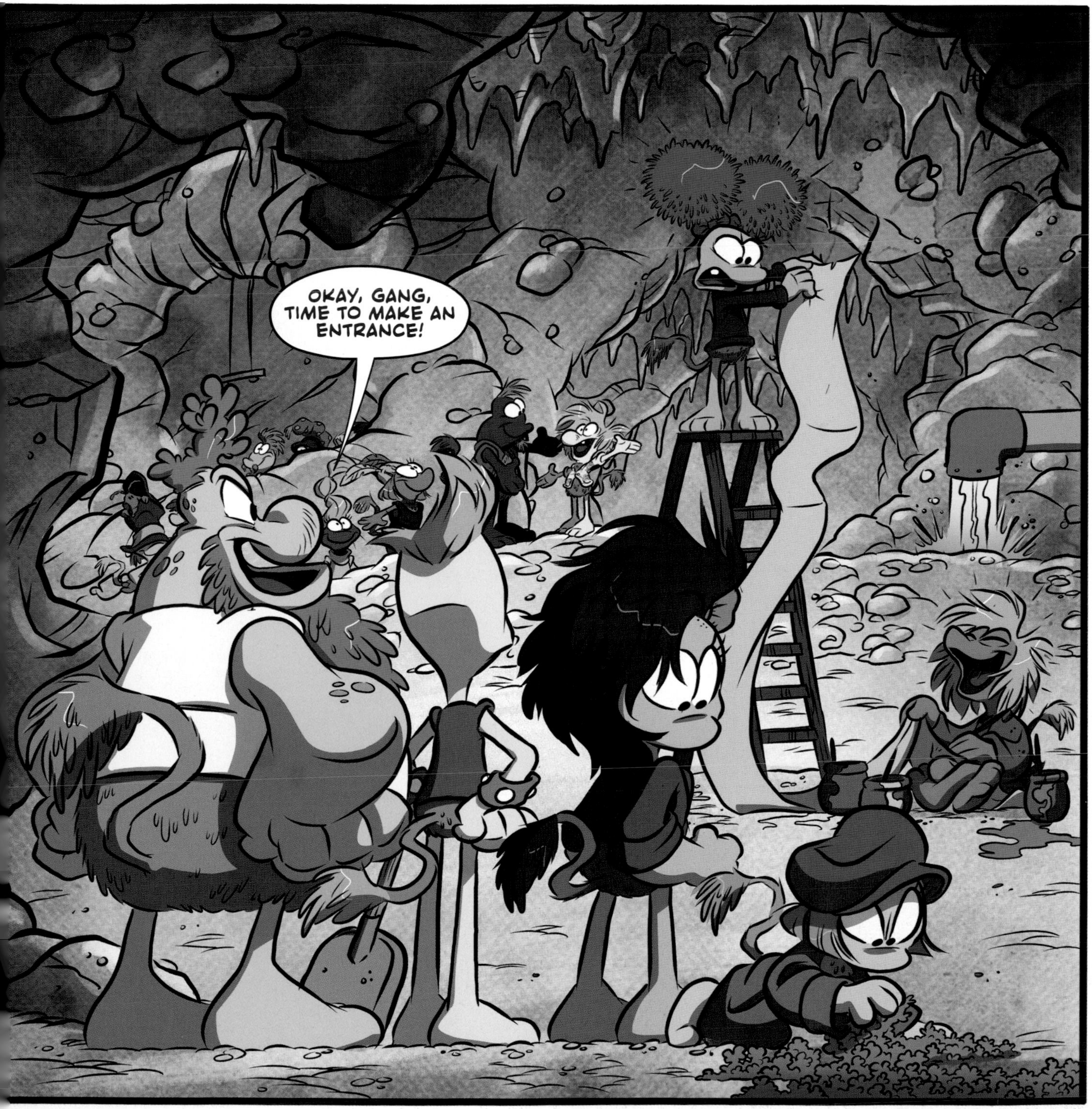
OKAY, GANG, TIME TO MAKE AN ENTRANCE!

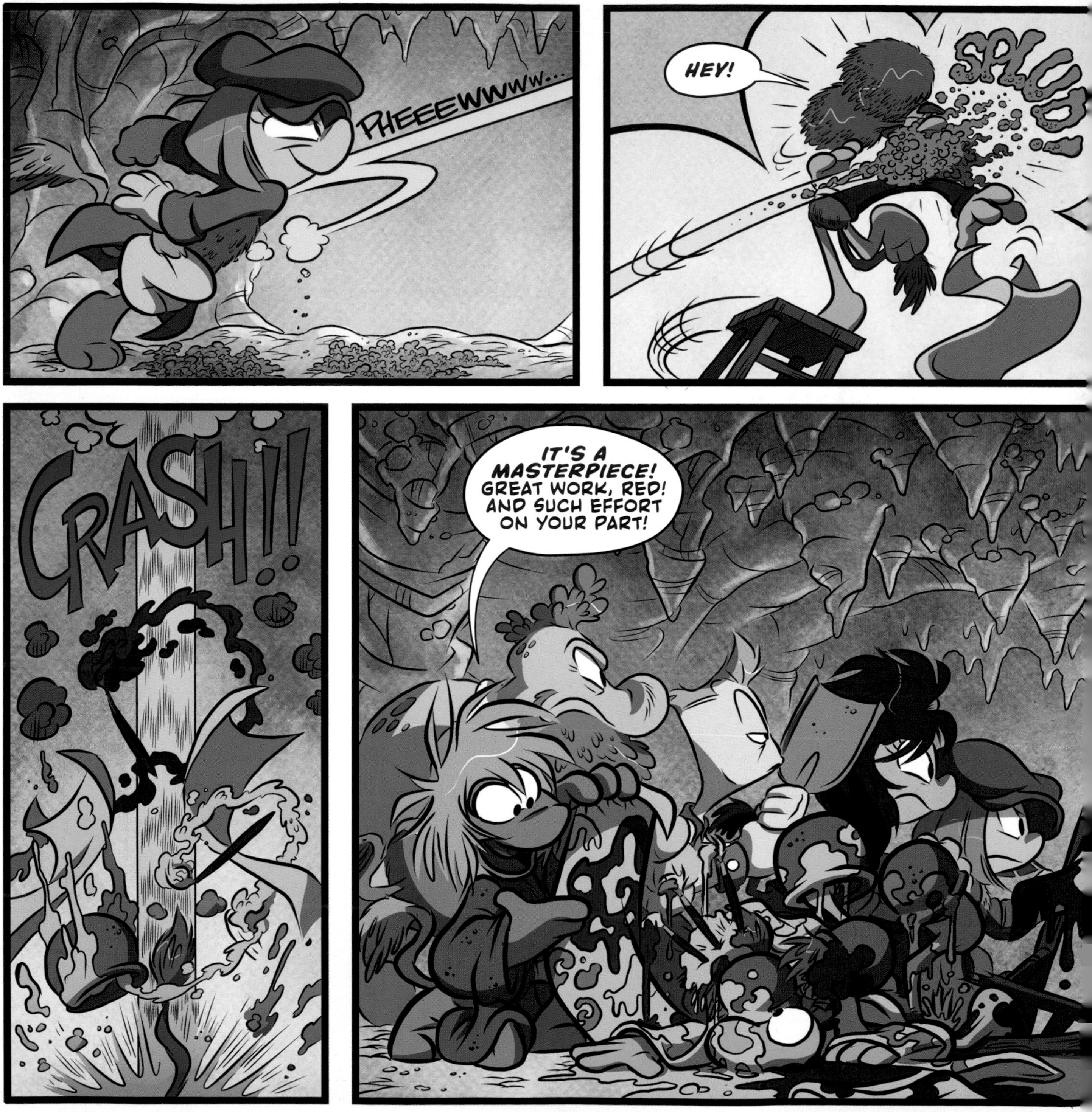
PHEEEWWWW...
HEY!
SPLUD!
CRASH!!
IT'S A MASTERPIECE! GREAT WORK, RED! AND SUCH EFFORT ON YOUR PART!

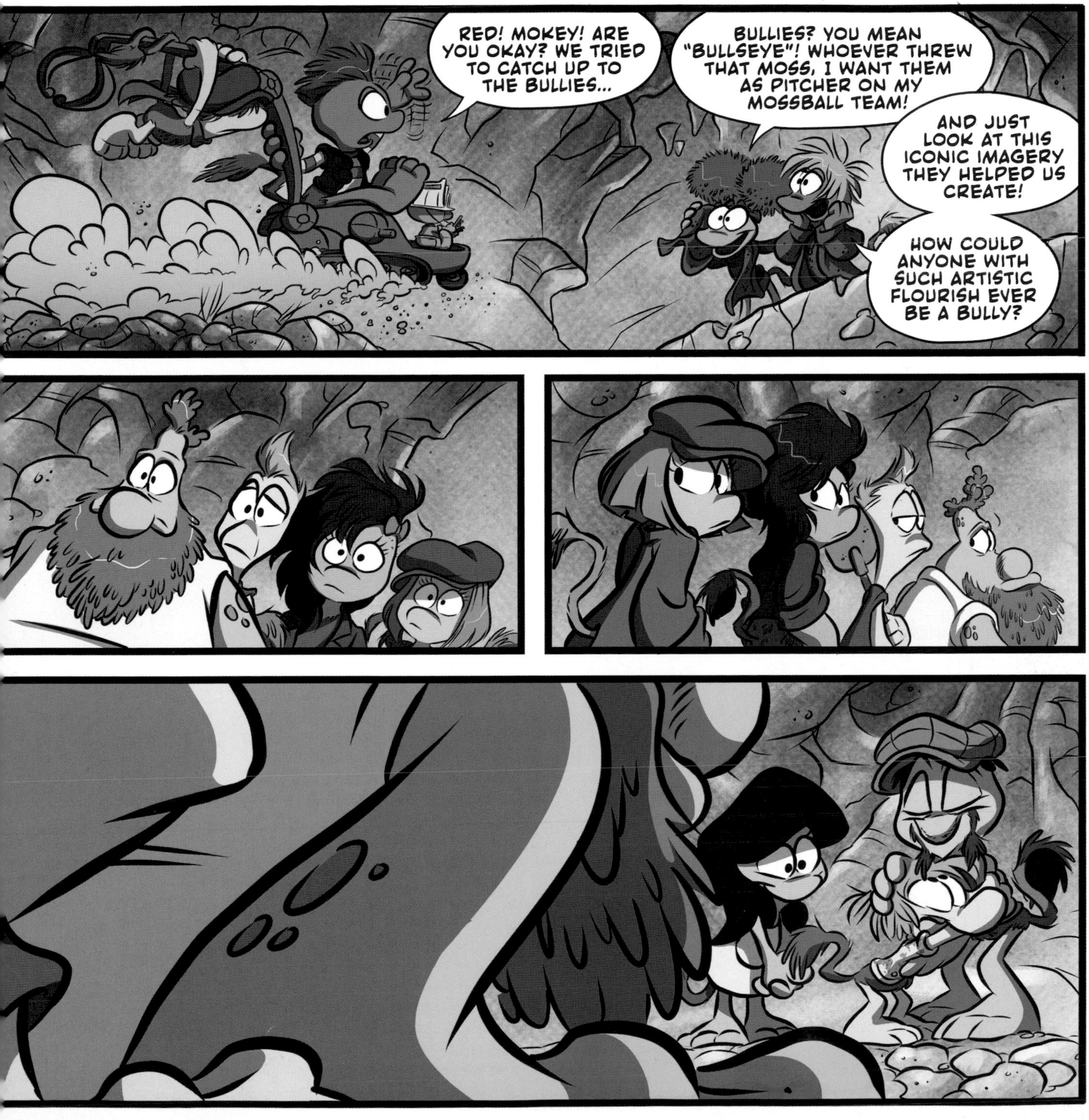
RED! MOKEY! ARE YOU OKAY? WE TRIED TO CATCH UP TO THE BULLIES...
BULLIES? YOU MEAN "BULLSEYE"! WHOEVER THREW THAT MOSS, I WANT THEM AS PITCHER ON MY MOSSBALL TEAM!
AND JUST LOOK AT THIS ICONIC IMAGERY THEY HELPED US CREATE!
HOW COULD ANYONE WITH SUCH ARTISTIC FLOURISH EVER BE A BULLY?

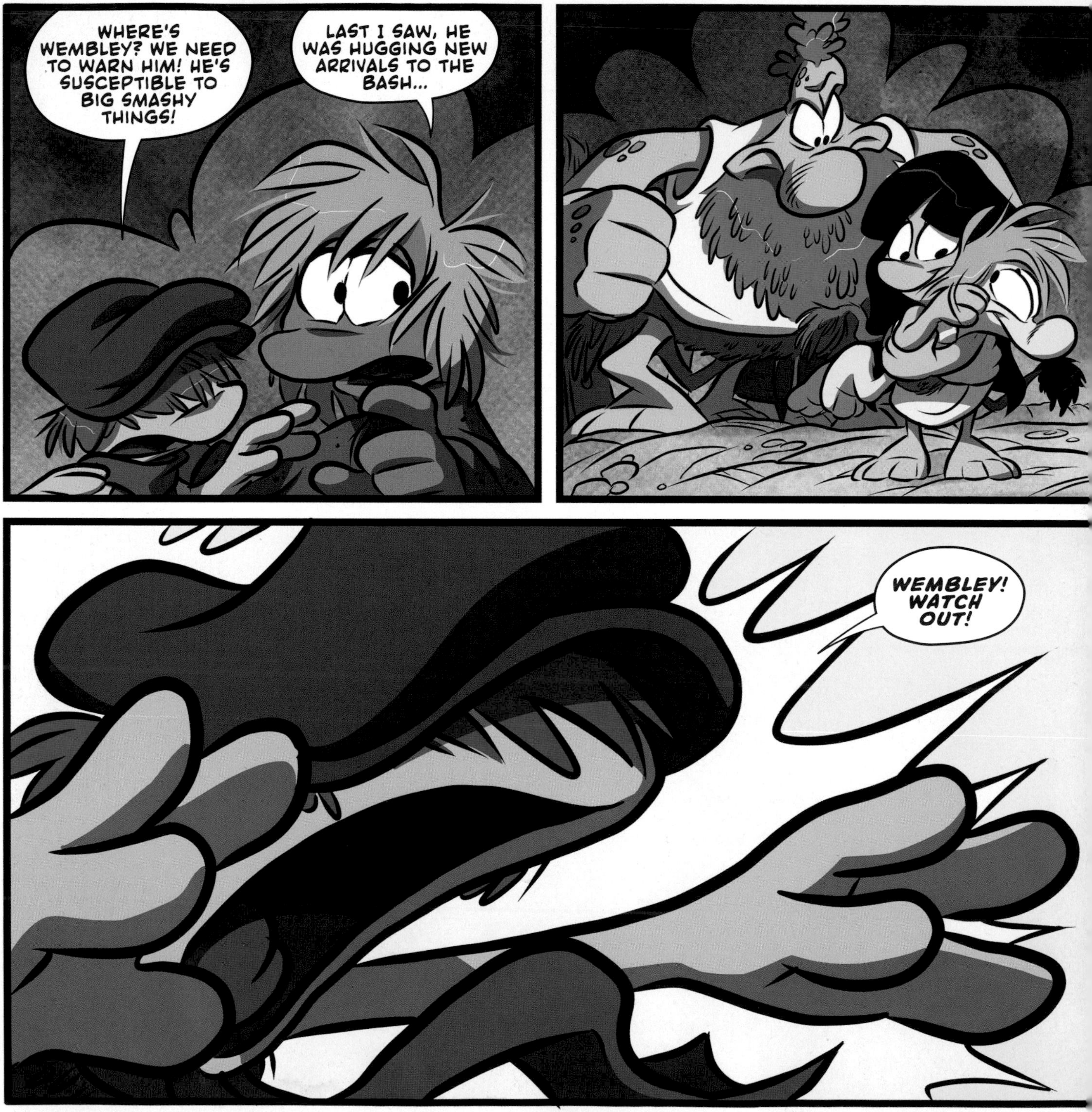
WHERE'S WEMBLEY? WE NEED TO WARN HIM! HE'S SUSCEPTIBLE TO BIG SMASHY THINGS!
LAST I SAW, HE WAS HUGGING NEW ARRIVALS TO THE BASH...
WEMBLEY! WATCH OUT!

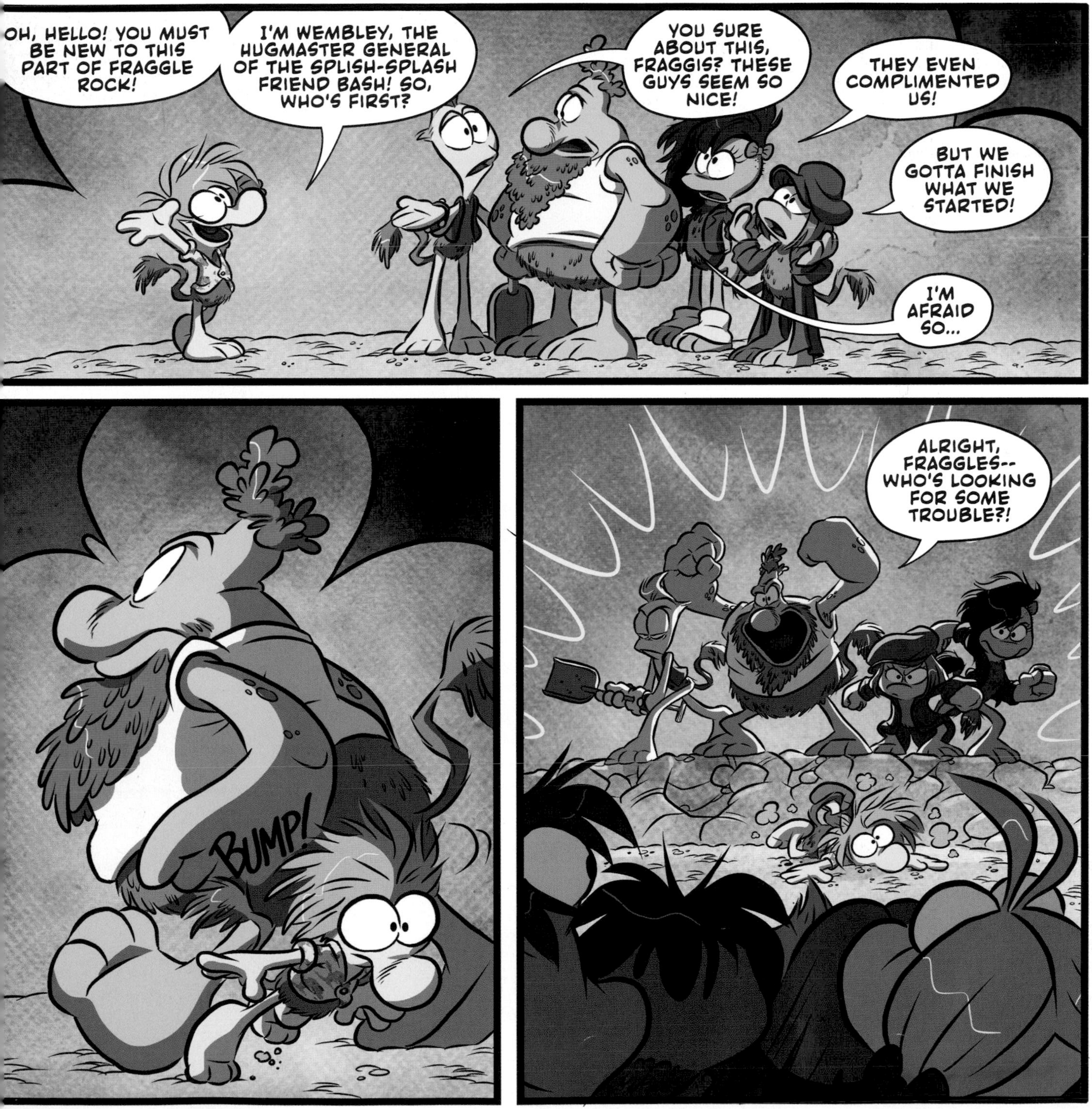
OH, HELLO! YOU MUST BE NEW TO THIS PART OF FRAGGLE ROCK!
I'M WEMBLEY, THE HUGMASTER GENERAL OF THE SPLISH-SPLASH FRIEND BASH! SO, WHO'S FIRST?
YOU SURE ABOUT THIS, FRAGGIS? THESE GUYS SEEM SO NICE!
THEY EVEN COMPLIMENTED US!
BUT WE GOTTA FINISH WHAT WE STARTED!
I'M AFRAID SO...
BUMP!
ALRIGHT, FRAGGLES-- WHO'S LOOKING FOR SOME TROUBLE?!

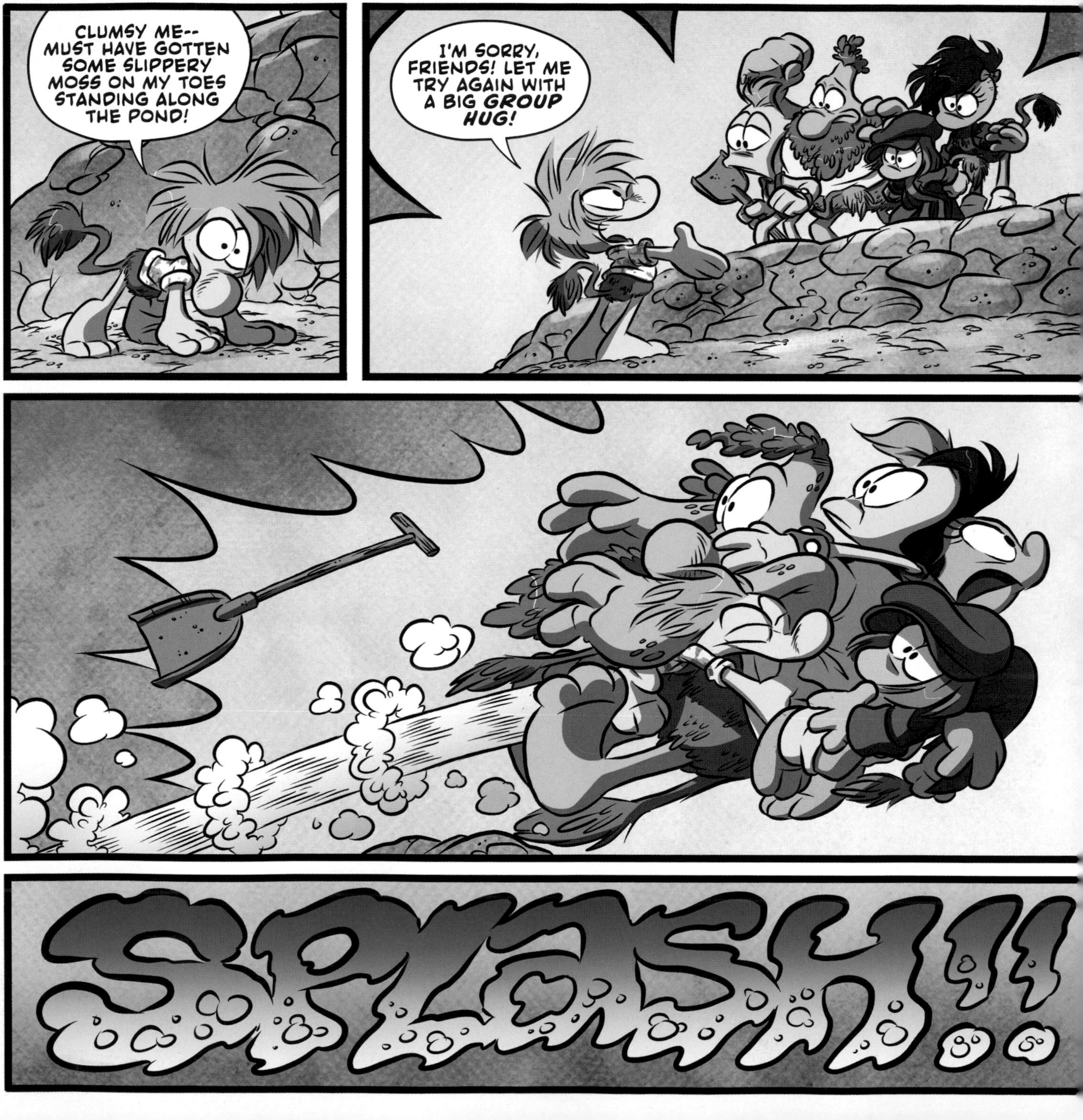
CLUMSY ME--MUST HAVE GOTTEN SOME SLIPPERY MOSS ON MY TOES STANDING ALONG THE POND!
I'M SORRY, FRIENDS! LET ME TRY AGAIN WITH A BIG GROUP HUG!
SPLASH!!

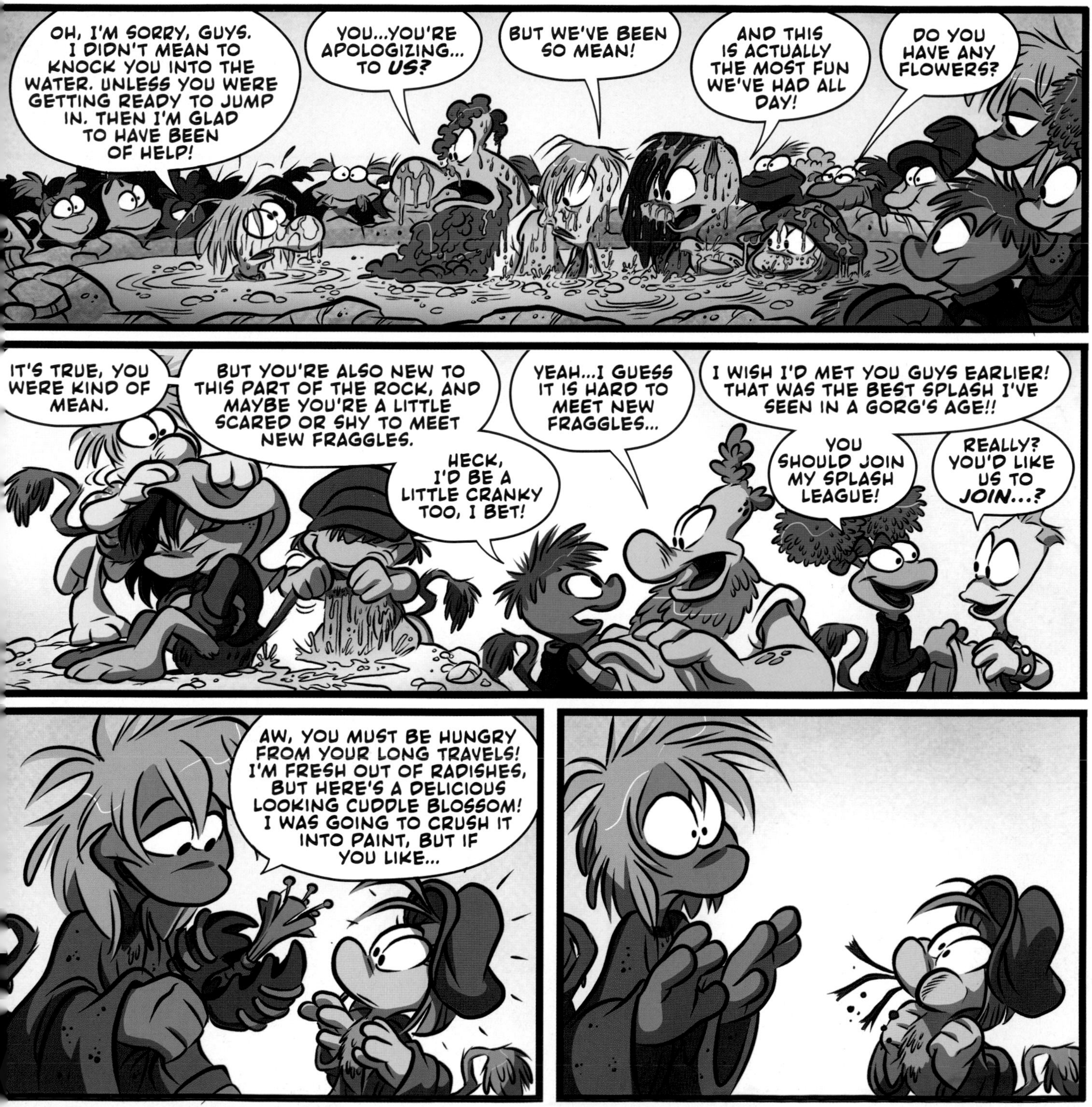
OH, I'M SORRY, GUYS. I DIDN'T MEAN TO KNOCK YOU INTO THE WATER. UNLESS YOU WERE GETTING READY TO JUMP IN. THEN I'M GLAD TO HAVE BEEN OF HELP!
YOU...YOU'RE APOLOGIZING... TO US?
BUT WE'VE BEEN SO MEAN!
AND THIS IS ACTUALLY THE MOST FUN WE'VE HAD ALL DAY!
DO YOU HAVE ANY FLOWERS?
IT'S TRUE, YOU WERE KIND OF MEAN.
BUT YOU'RE ALSO NEW TO THIS PART OF THE ROCK, AND MAYBE YOU'RE A LITTLE SCARED OR SHY TO MEET NEW FRAGGLES.
HECK, I'D BE A LITTLE CRANKY TOO, I BET!
YEAH...I GUESS IT IS HARD TO MEET NEW FRAGGLES...
I WISH I'D MET YOU GUYS EARLIER! THAT WAS THE BEST SPLASH I'VE SEEN IN A GORG'S AGE!!
YOU SHOULD JOIN MY SPLASH LEAGUE!
REALLY? YOU'D LIKE US TO JOIN...?
AW, YOU MUST BE HUNGRY FROM YOUR LONG TRAVELS! I'M FRESH OUT OF RADISHES, BUT HERE'S A DELICIOUS LOOKING CUDDLE BLOSSOM! I WAS GOING TO CRUSH IT INTO PAINT, BUT IF YOU LIKE...

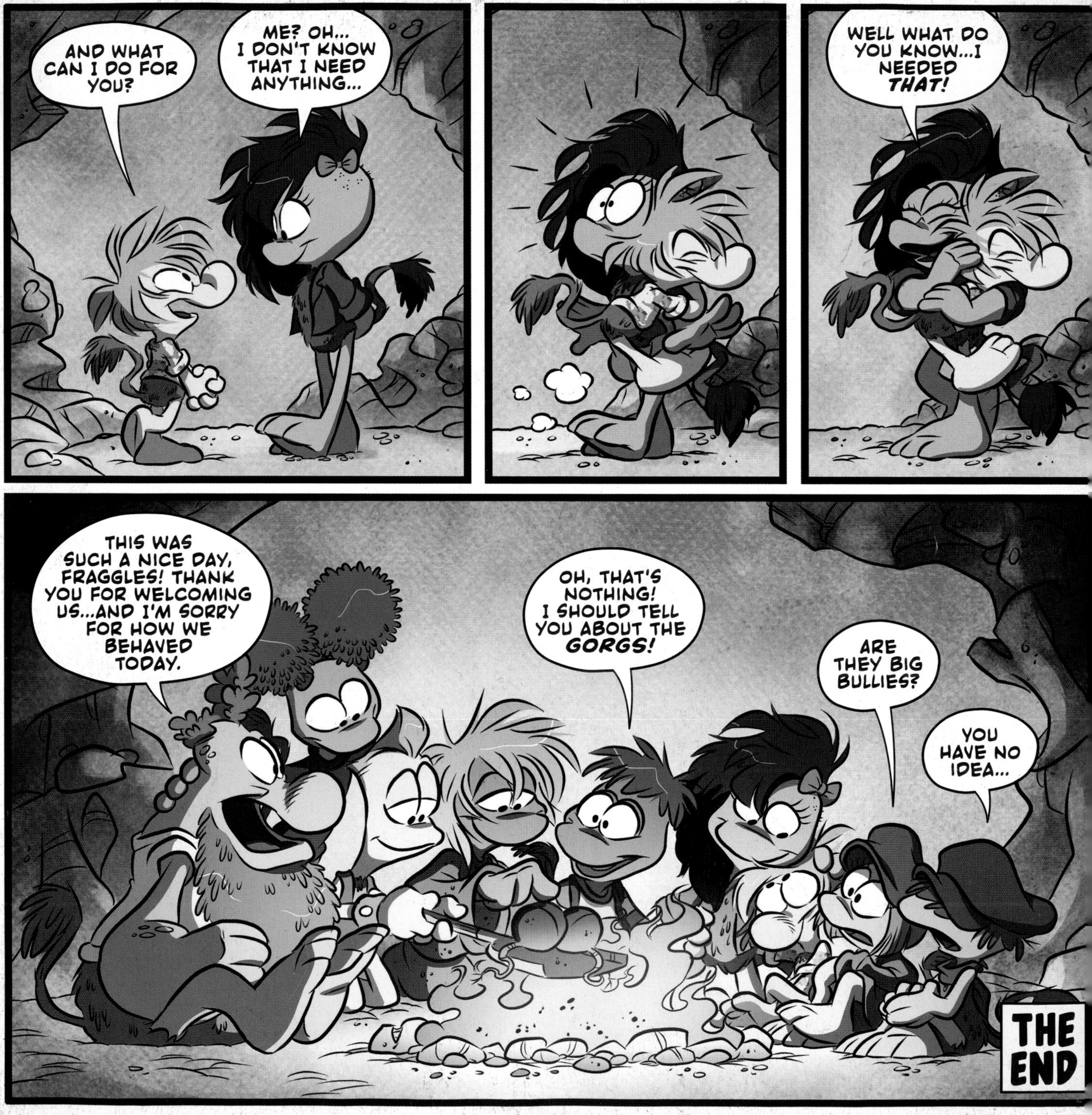
AND WHAT CAN I DO FOR YOU?
ME? OH... I DON'T KNOW THAT I NEED ANYTHING...
WELL WHAT DO YOU KNOW...I NEEDED THAT!
THIS WAS SUCH A NICE DAY, FRAGGLES! THANK YOU FOR WELCOMING US...AND I'M SORRY FOR HOW WE BEHAVED TODAY.
OH, THAT'S NOTHING! I SHOULD TELL YOU ABOUT THE GORGS!
ARE THEY BIG BULLIES?
YOU HAVE NO IDEA...
THE END

DISCOVER
THE WORLD OF JIM HENSON

Jim Henson's
TALE OF SAND
The lost screenplay by JIM HENSON and JERRY JUHL
As realized by RAMÓN K. PÉREZ

Jim Henson's
LABYRINTH
ARTIST TRIBUTE

Jim Henson's
THE POWER OF THE
DARK CRYSTAL
Simon Spurrier
Kelly Matthews
Nichole Matthews

Jim Henson's
THE STORYTELLER
Dragons

The Dark Crystal
TALES

Jim Henson's
LABYRINTH
ADULT COLORING BOOK

ARCHAIA™

AVAILABLE AT YOUR LOCAL COMICS SHOP AND BOOKSTORE

WWW.**BOOM-STUDIOS**.COM

Jim Henson's Tale of Sand
Jim Henson, Jerry Juhl, Ramón K. Pérez
ISBN: 978-1-93639-309-1 | $29.95 US

Jim Henson's The Dark Crystal: Creation Myths
Brian Froud, Alex Sheikman, Joshua Dysart, and others
Volume 1
ISBN: 978-1-60886-704-2 | $14.99 US
Volume 2
ISBN: 978-1-60886-887-2 | $14.99 US
Volume 3
ISBN: 978-1-60886-906-0 | $14.99 US

Jim Henson's The Power of the Dark Crystal
Simon Spurrier, Kelly and Nichole Matthews
Volume 1
ISBN: 978-1-60886-992-3 | $24.99 US

Jim Henson's The Dark Crystal Tales
Cory Godbey
ISBN: 978-1-60886-845-2 | $16.99 US

Jim Henson's Labyrinth Artist Tribute
Michael Allred, Dave McKean, Faith Erin Hicks, and others
ISBN: 978-1-60886-897-1 | $24.99 US

Jim Henson's Labyrinth Adult Coloring Book
Jorge Corona, Jay Fosgitt, Phil Murphy
ISBN: 978-1-68415-111-0 | $16.99 US

Jim's Henson's The Musical Monsters of Turkey Hollow
Jim Henson, Jerry Juhl, Roger Langridge
ISBN: 978-1-60886-434-8 | $24.99 US

Jim Henson's The Storyteller: Witches
S.M. Vidaurri, Kyla Vanderklugt, Matthew Dow Smith, Jeff Stokely
ISBN: 978-1-60886-747-9 | $24.99 US

Jim Henson's The Storyteller: Dragons
Daniel Bayliss, Jorge Corona,
Hannah Christensen, Nathan Pride
ISBN: 978-1-60886-874-2 | $24.99 US

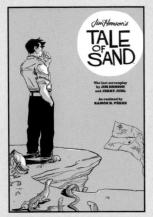

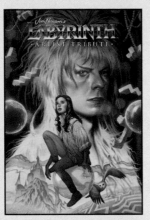

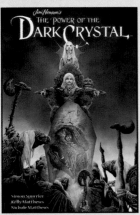

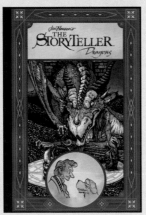

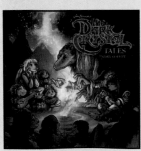

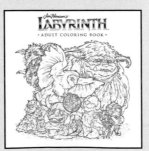

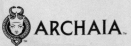